Shackles of Doubt

Book Two of the Calypto Cycle

The Calypto Cycle

Fire in the Snow
Shackles of Doubt
Threads Unravel (forthcoming in 2018)

Shackles of Doubt

D. Thomas Minton

Copyright © 2017 D. Thomas Minton
Cover art by Hans Binder Knott © 2017
Cover design by Holly Heisey

This book is available in print and electronic formats and at most online retailers.

ISBN: 0998304239
ISBN-13: 978-0-9983042-3-6

This one is for Jenn

PART I

ALL GOOD THINGS

I EAT THE LAST WEDGE of cheese, leaving behind a few crumbs on the porcelain saucer. The cheese is mildly nutty and creamy, and if this were another time, another place, I would have savored it, but today, I cannot let myself get lost in the simple pleasure.

Not while I'm being watched.

My shadow, wearing a light jacket to ward off the cool breeze, sits along the quayside pretending to read a newspaper. With too much regularity, he lowers it as he methodically turns the page, and in that moment, casually glances about, but always in my direction. His hat, pulled low, shades his eyes, but does not conceal his close-cropped beard and a nose like a cleaver.

I first noticed him last night while heading back to my room after an early dinner. His hard shoes had clicked on the uneven sidewalk in time to my steps. Likely, he was unaware that the configuration of the buildings on Tanev's narrow streets amplified the noise as well as the Beleshkov Theatre in Aurestapol. At first the shoes were simply background noise, barely noticeable among the music spilling from the clubs and the clatter of outdoor diners, but when I stopped at cross streets, so too did the shoes. When I halted experimentally at a haberdashery to admire the latest styles in its window, so too did the shoes. When I turned, so did the shoes. So I walked him around for a while until I could get a surreptitious look at him—the same close-cropped beard, the same nose as the man with the newspaper.

I drain the last of my espresso and deliberately return the cup to its saucer. I'm not in any immediate danger. I know that because of my Talent. Ordinary people talk about Talent as a natural gift of skill, whether it is with a football, or paint brush, or trouble. My Talent is similar, yet different. I see the future ... sort of. What really happens is that I sense when things are about to go dangerously wrong for me. It manifests itself in a sense of vertigo, like the gears and cogs of the world have come out of alignment for a brief second, before falling back into place and lurching forward. In that briefest of moments, I've learned I can react—that I must react—if I'm to avoid whatever fate is sending my way.

Seated here at the café table, I sense nothing. I have already concluded that my shadow isn't here to physically bring me harm. At least not yet. He's here to watch, and if he wasn't such an amateur, I'd likely never have noticed him.

Almost on cue, the newspaper lowers, and the man's eyes rove to the left then back past me as he turns the pages of the paper and raises it once again.

A few meters from where I sit, a couple strolls along the sand admiring the slate gray waters of the

Dardan Sea. We're around a small point from the harbor, so our view is unobstructed to the horizon where the deep blue sky kisses the water's surface. Based on the couple's age and stylish coats, they are an officer and his girl on leave from the front. Regular enlistments can't afford Tanev.

Looking out across the water, I can almost forget the war, the shortages and the hardships of the Empire, but to my right, the Battleship Tsurov sits at anchor, a hulking steel monument to violence. Smoke from its triple stacks smudges the otherwise unblemished sky like a fly smeared on a tablecloth.

I run my finger along the lip of my cup, wondering again to whom my shadow is reporting. The Red Cuffs? Possibly. Most people quake at the thought of the Ministry for State Security taking any interest in them, but since El Emir, I've become accustomed to their scrutiny. They may be brutally efficient at rooting out the Empire's traitors, dissidents, and other unsavory elements, but shadowing requires subtle skill, something wholly lacking from the average Red Cuff repertoire.

He could be part of the Silver Tigers, a shadow group I encountered for the first time two weeks ago. Revolutionaries, I think, but I know little about them except they are dangerous. They don't strike me as the type to sit and watch, though.

I find it odd that my first thought has not been the Papalate, our antagonists across the no-man's land in this brutal war. Or perhaps the Quin, our neighbors to the east, who have little love for the Empire—a level of affection that goes both ways. Perhaps it's a bit vain to think I would ever be important enough for their attention, but my missions for The Order have certainly caused both nations problems.

The waitress smiles at me as she places my check near my elbow. If my life wasn't so complicated, I might have found her slender face and long neck attractive, and maybe even tried to strike up a conversation, but my life doesn't have room for that kind of normalcy—something I've learned the hard way.

Regret stabs at my ribs, and for a moment I find it hard to breathe. Only recently I learned I have a ten-year old daughter. Odella, her mother, had kept her a secret from me, and only through an accident of chance did I learn of her. Odella had no right to do that, even if I understand why she did it.

Men like me aren't good fathers. Better we're dead than simply absent. Still, to not even be deemed worthy of knowing, hurts.

That's what happens when people like me think we can have something normal.

I drop a few coins on the table and head out into the street, pretending not to notice my shadow tuck his folded paper under his arm and rise to follow.

It's mid-afternoon, and the streets of Tanev are quiet. Few in the Empire can afford a holiday during these difficult times, and the military officers who make up the majority of the clientele are either frolicking on the beach or recovering from a night of carousing. Neither activity appeals to me.

I am a reluctant tourist, courtesy of R, my handler in The Order.

Almost getting killed makes people think you need time off to recover, but I've waltzed with death before; she's no strange dance partner. And this last brush was minor—a wound to my right leg that is now nothing more than a circle of new pink skin. This forced convalescence is more about getting me out the way, I think, so I can't ask questions. In Tanev, my questions fester like an open wound. I don't like having so much time to think. Thinking is an operative's most hazardous activity.

My shadow's shoes pad softly behind me, quieter today than they were last night, but probably he is being more cautious because the streets are empty this afternoon, except for the two of us.

Tanev has cobblestone streets with narrow sidewalks and buildings that look individually hand-built instead of die-cast like the Empire's more recent, industrial towns. Nearly as old as Aurestapol, Tanev dates to before the Emperor's line ascended to the White Throne. It was intended as a playground for the noble families, and many of the buildings look like those you'd find in the more reputable neighborhoods of Aurestapol proper, only in miniature and with rustic trappings in the wooden accents and crafted wrought iron fixtures. Autos aren't allowed in the city center, so the place feels like I've stepped through a doorway to a hundred years ago.

Ahead, sitting on a stoop, a man in white shirt watches my approach. As I near, he rises and flashes something in his hand: a cigarette tucked between his fingers.

"Spare a light?" He motions again with his cigarette hand. Nestled in his palm is a matchbook such that only I can see it.

"Sure, sure," I say, patting my pockets. He's caught me off guard, and I fumble for a little time while I study his clean-shaven face. I've not seen him before; he's very young, a fresh recruit into whatever scheme he's working today. He's barely legal age, I would guess, but he's playing his part with a calm that suggests more experience than his baby-face implies.

I have no matches. I don't smoke, but I pretend to draw out a matchbook. My fumbling around gives the man time to move his cigarette to lips where he leaves it dangling. As we make the mock transfer, he flips the matchbook from his palm into is fingers and holds it up, like a magician completing his illusion. Anyone watching would be convinced I gave it to him. He tears away a match and scrapes it across the back of the book. The match flares brightly, smelling of sulfur. Bluish smoke trails from the corner of his mouth, and the cigarette tip glows like a fanned ember. He exhales to the side so as not to blow smoke into my face.

"I needed that," he says with a smile. I can't immediately place his accent, not that it matters, because I doubt it's his true manner of speech. He hands the matchbook to me, and I stuff it into my pocket without looking at it.

"Thank you." He motions with the cigarette as if he needs to explain his gratitude then he sits down again, and takes pleasure in his smoke.

I continue on my way.

Several blocks later, I notice my shadow again. Likely he has circled around to avoid walking past the cigarette man. Maybe he's not as much an amateur as I originally thought. If he's no amateur, maybe he wants me to know I'm being watched, which I suspect is something a Red Cuff would do, thinking his presence would unsettle his target. For ordinary people that's true, and as the thought occurs to me now, it does put more of a knot in my stomach than usual, but nothing that would ever give me pause.

I reach my guesthouse and return to my room. It's nothing fancy—a square room slightly larger than that to which I'm accustomed, a firm bed with stiff sheets, and a chair in the corner that catches the morning sun through the room's only window. The window looks out onto a small courtyard with vine-covered trellises and a pair of benches. I've not been down to it.

I lock the door, and pull the curtains shut. They're sheer and let enough light into the room, but keep out prying eyes.

I fish the matchbook from my pocket. Printed on the cover is a cat in a top hat and bow tie. In yellow script is the name "Club Hat Cat." A stupid name for a club, but I've seen it in my wanderings—a small place in a walk down a short distance from my room. Written inside the cover is the number 1830, which I assume is a time. The handwriting is sloppy, as if someone took care to make sure it could not be easily traced back to its author. I peel the matches back looking for more information, but find nothing. Satisfied there is no more to learn, I tear free a match and set the book on fire, turning it carefully to ensure that it is entirely consumed. Before it burns my fingers, I drop it into the toilet. It sizzles as it goes out, leaving a spreading puddle of ash on the surface of the water. I flush it down.

I crack open the window to let out the smell of the burned matchbook.

I check my pocket watch, and snap it closed. It's early still. I have nothing to do but wait. And think.

今

FROM THE CHAIR, I watch the sky darken—pale blue to cerulean to eggplant to something that resembles a bruise—until stars poke through the night. The only light seeps under the crack beneath my door from the hallway.

Is my shadow still out there, or has he given up?

Watching a dark room must drain the will.

I change my shirt and strap on my FP's shoulder holster. The cartridge of flechettes is full, and clicks coldly as I push it back into place. The holster sits snugly under my right arm, angled so the FP's stubby handle projects forward for easy access. Once I pull on my suit coat, the gun is invisible to all but the most scrutinizing eye. In the dark, I knot my tie by feel. I even close my eyes and savor the tactile sense of wrapping and tucking the silk. The knot slides snugly to my throat.

My watch says it's time to go. I slip on my long jacket. I've not needed it during Tanev's mild winter days, but this is the first night I've gone out, and while I don't plan to be gone long, one never knows what unexpected meetings may bring.

My room is on the second floor, and I presume the only door out of the guesthouse is being watched. At the end of the hallway is a window that opens onto a fire escape that drops into a narrow alley along the side of the building. The window sticks and makes noise as I wrench it open wide enough to step out. Fortunately, no one seems to hear, or more likely, isn't interested in investigating. The fire ladder down into the alley doesn't look like it's ever been lowered, so I leave it be. I climb over the railing and lower myself until I can drop quietly to the cobblestones. There, I freeze in a crouch, listening to the sounds from the street—faint voices, but nothing approaching. I head in the opposite direction.

The other end of the alley opens onto a quiet avenue of row houses. With the blackout cloths pulled over the windows, they are featureless shadows. The stars give enough light to navigate the narrow, unevenly paved lane. After several turns, I arrive at Club Hat Cat.

A scattering of people fills the place, but given the club's limited size and the thickness of the cigarette smoke, it feels nearly full. The yellowish light cast from the low-wattage wall lamps gives everything the sepia glow of a stained photograph. A bar runs along the side wall, just inside the door. Small, round tables fill the cramped space between the bar stools and a low, wooden stage in the back corner. The stage is cluttered with four chairs, metal stands for sheet music, and instrument cases.

Sweat beads instantly prickle my brow.

I don't know who I'm meeting, but I assume whoever he is will find me.

"Welcome, welcome," the man behind the bar calls out to me. He waves me forward. "What do you want, friend? I've got the finest vodka in the Empire. No? Wine then. Red?"

When I don't respond to any of his offers, he continues to rattle off drinks as he sets a plate on the bar and stocks it with a few slices of pickled beet, a single pancake with a scoop of roe on the side, as well as several slivers of smoked ham, not once taking his eyes off me. While he does that, I slowly scan the faces in the club, but they are hard to make out in the hazy light.

"Vodka," I say finally, and the barman falls quiet, but smoothly produces a glass that he fills halfway.

"Keep the rest," I say, putting a coin on the counter.

Grinning, he collects the coin and moves away.

I check my watch. I'm right on time. I would expect my party to—

A hand waves at me from the far side of the room.

This is it. I squeeze my right arm against my body; the slender bulk of my FP presses reassuringly into my ribs. Deciding to take my drink, I reluctantly leave the plate of *zakuski* on the bar, so as to keep my pistol hand free. The noise in the room seems to get sucked away as my focus narrows on the squat form at the table, but in the dim, smoky light, I can't make out any details of his face. As I cross the room, I am acutely aware of every muscle in every limb and the feeling in my gut. I'm ready to react if my Talent gives any indication that something is wrong, but I reach the table without any incident.

"You lost your friend, I assume?"

I nearly drop my drink, but I shouldn't be

surprised.

The chair across from R slides away from the table as she pushes it toward me with her foot.

I slide the wooden chair around so its back is toward the wall then settle into it. I'm happy to find a half-full vodka bottle and a plate of cheese, crepes, and pickled beets.

"You know about him?" Of course she does. Even though I'm relatively sure R is human, she has a knack for being omniscient. It's one of her many traits that make her a good handler, and has kept me alive. "Do you know who he is?"

She lightly taps the cuff of her blouse, confirming my initial suspicion. "Have you been enjoying the sea air? I hear it's good for the health."

The corners of my lips rise slightly. I'm not used small talk from R.

Other than a handful of field agents and the people who trained me, R is the only person I know in The Order. Considering she's been my handler since I was recruited many years ago, I know relatively little about her. Most of our meetings are short, to the point, and occur with an efficiency of words and actions.

"How's your arm?" I ask.

Reflexively she touches her right shoulder, drawing attention to the bulky harness under her blouse. The last time I saw her, the arm had been in a sling. At that meeting she had refused to answer my questions; instead she gave me a ticket to Tanev. Obedient as always, I took it.

"It's good," she says.

"And Lera?" I lower my eyes so she won't see how much I want her to answer that question. I haven't seen Lera since the night in the park, when R took the flechettes, and Lera took much worse. In that meeting with R, before I departed for Tanev, she only told me Lera would be fine. Her curt response made plain that it wasn't a topic for discussion.

"She's well," R says. "She started her training, and from what I hear, is proving a formidable challenge." Her grin is enigmatic.

Under R's elbow is a manila envelope. She slides it to the center of the table, leaving it next to the plate of *zakuski*.

"I thought I was on holiday." My voice is edged with sarcasm.

"All good things must come to an end."

I leave the envelope where it sits. It's not mine yet, and I feel like a trained dog waiting for my command so I can do my trick and get my reward.

"I don't want you in the field yet," R says, and I sense genuine concern in her tone. "But my wants are unimportant in times like this."

"I'm tired of sitting around. I don't take to it."

"Of course you don't." Her expression doesn't change as she watches me. I'm not sure if she's taking a playful jab at me, or simply making plain that she knows me as well—or likely better—than I know myself.

"I tried to get this one assigned to someone else, but command was clear that this was your mission. To be honest, I don't know why. It's not your skill set. There are two dozen operatives better suited for this one."

R's lack of faith in me stings, even if she is probably right. Her job is to get results from her agents. She knows my every strength and weakness, but her telling me this is surprising. She's never questioned those above her in my presence before, so why now?

"Why me, then?"

R starts to shrug then seems to reconsider. "They must see something I don't."

My mouth pulls down into a frown.

"Don't take that the wrong way, Calypto," she says. "You're good at what you do. If you weren't, you wouldn't be here."

I'm not sure if she means I wouldn't be part of The Order, or I wouldn't be alive. She could mean both, I suppose, because I realize those two conditions are not mutually exclusive. If I wasn't part of The Order, I likely wouldn't be alive today. The Order rescued me from the Empire's protective care system, where upon reaching age seventeen, unclaimed boys are enlisted into the army as a way to repay their debt to the state. I doubt I would have lasted long in the army, especially on the front where even my Talent would be of little use against mustard gas, aerial shellings, and dysentery.

I down my vodka to fill the silence with something other than my thoughts. The liquor is smooth and dry and burns a warm path to my stomach. It is every bit as good as the barman boasted. I pour another and top off R's glass.

She nods toward the envelope. I slide it to me and pull at the string that holds the flap shut. While I do this, R lowers her voice to thwart anyone attempting to listen. "We have identified a spy who has been passing information on troop movements to the Papalate. Your job is to apprehend him."

"That sounds like work for the Red Cuffs, not us."

R gives me a weak smile that tells me she agrees, but that the matter is not in her hands.

"We are not sure we have identified the right person," she says, "and that is where things get delicate, and likely why this matter came to us and not the Red Cuffs."

I nod. The Ministry of State Security uses sledgehammers to extract splinters, but that has never stopped them in the past. "Who?" I ask.

"Arkady Petrescu."

My lips curve into a round oh, and my breath whistles faintly through them. "Big fish."

Petrescu heads the only other family with a legitimate claim to the throne. If things had gone differently a century ago, Arkady Petrescu would be seated in the White Palace. The Petrescu family has never fully accepted the twist of historical fate that left them the bridesmaid, although from everything I've heard, Arkady Petrescu has always been a loyal servant to the Empire. He had led the charge that had turned back the Papalate forces at the Khyber twenty years ago during the St. Nicholas Day Conflict. His bravery crushed the Papalate's will, and many believe his actions were directly responsible for getting them to the negotiating table. Cowed, they ceded key territory in the Dardenees. Petrescu even served on the front during the early years of this most recent conflict, taking a shell fragment that nearly killed him. Unable to continue, he reluctantly retired from service. What he was doing now, I could not say, but this was not the record of traitor, which only made it even more likely.

"His dossier?" I raise the envelope.

She nods, a shallow tilt of her head. "Inside, along

with a train ticket, and some cash. When you get to Coruşu, you will make contact with Mélon. He will have additional instructions for you."

"How will I know him?"

"He will find you, and the pass code is in with the dossier."

I grunt softly. I don't like having to rely on others to complete my missions. What if this Mélon fails to find me, then what do I do? When you put your faith in others, you are only setting yourself up for disappointment at best, and catastrophic failure at worst.

"Mélon will be there," R says, as if reading my thoughts. She nods toward the *zakuski*. "Try the *varenye*."

I take the last pancake and smear it with sour cream and globs of strawberry *varenye*. As I do so, my mouth waters, and I realize I haven't eaten anything since this morning. I force myself to take a small bite. The pancake is so-so, but the *varenye* is sweet and flavorful. My mouth aches. I finish the pancake and stuff in a chunk of hard yellow cheese followed by one of the beets.

"You need to take better care of yourself," R says.

I force myself to sit back in the chair. Slowly I chew and swallow the food. R's face looks unusual in the dim light, and it takes me several moments to realize something is troubling her. She is withholding information, but not without a struggle. I've never seen her like this before, and given the foreignness of this territory, I don't know what to do. Then, in a flash, the expression that makes her look uncertain, almost vulnerable, is gone, and the R I have always known is back—an R in command of every muscle, every expression.

"You better go. Your train leaves in less than an hour. Don't go back to your room."

"I never intended to," I say, rising.

"Be careful, Calypto," she says as I turn away.

The only other time she's given me that warning, the mission nearly killed me.

今

A SMALL KNOT OF PEOPLE mills outside Club Hat
Cat; I'm unsure whether they are waiting to go in or
have come out of the smoke to catch clean air, but
none of them pays me any attention as I slip through
them and head down the street. After a few turns to
confirm I've not picked up a shadow, I head to the
train.

Tanev's station isn't large, but the interior feels
empty because only a single train, westbound for
Kovrov, leaves tonight. The passengers are an odd
mixture of wealthy aristocrats heading home to
Aurestapol and officers re-deploying back to the
western front. If their clothing hadn't so obviously
distinguished the two, I wouldn't have been able to
tell one group from the other; both wear equally grave
expressions, even if one group is returning to
restricted heating fuel and sugar rations, and the other
likely heading off to their deaths.

By contrast, I have a spring in my step as I board
the train. Tanev may be a fine city, but I never wanted
to be here. In many ways, the down time has been

harder than being on a mission. I'm not addicted to danger—I don't want to be visited by harm any more than any other citizen—but being on a mission gives me purpose and focus. I don't have the luxury to think about anything other than the task at hand, and, in many cases, staying alive.

Once in my compartment, I lock the door and pull its window shade before settling onto the bench. The brown envelope I set on the cushion next to me, and allow myself a moment to relax. I realize then how quickly my heart is thumping, and that my forehead is beaded with sweat. I realize also that my Talent hasn't so much as tingled during my entire six days in Tanev.

My brow crinkles.

I'm not sure that's happened in my entire life, and I don't like it. My mind briefly spirals down into a panic-fueled scenario in which I no longer have my Talent. As a child, I wished many times that I hadn't been cursed with it. For a long time I believed it was the reason my parents had abandoned me and forced me into the state protective system. It was what made me different from the other children, and being scrawny and awkward and different is always tough for a child, especially one with no family to support him. Only as an adult did I realize my Talent was an integral part of who I am, as much as my face and knowledge and experiences coalesce to be me. To lose my Talent would be to lose part of who I am.

I take several deep breaths. My heart rate slows as I push away these ridiculous thoughts. This type of idle thinking doesn't happen when I'm on a mission, which is why I'm happy to be leaving Tanev.

Kovrov is seven hours away, but right now I'm too awake to sleep. I unstring the envelope and slide out several sheets of onion skin paper, a train ticket for my connection to Coruşu and a small stack of notes. The ticket and money I tuck into my suit coat pocket without counting it. I'm sure there is enough for my needs; there always is.

Clipped to the paper is a grainy picture of Arkady Petrescu and his wife, Catherine. It's a candid moment caught on the street at some sort of public event, based on the crowd in the background. While there is little frame of reference, Petrescu looks like a hulking bear of a man. His wild mane of dark hair is streaked with bolts of white, and I suspect it would fly about his head unheeded if he had not tamed it into a tail in the back. He towers over his wife, whose slender frame looks like it would be crushed in his arms, but there is hard resolution in her eyes. Unlike her husband, she is peering directly into the camera while the picture is taken, and from her eyes, I sense she knows she is being photographed, and that she is issuing a challenge to whoever might be viewing her picture in the future.

The thought gives me a shudder.

I set aside the photograph then study the text pounded into the flimsy paper.

Since leaving the Emperor's service three years ago, Petrescu has re-taken charge of the family business—DANSC Shipping—which was originally deeded to his family when the Imperial line ascended to the White Throne. DANSC moves food, clothing, medical supplies—everything as far as I can tell—directly to the troops on the Romani and Westari fronts, where the Empire's forces recently have been out maneuvered to devastating effect. Or so the mission dossier says, because news from the fronts, especially bad news, seldom reaches far into the Empire. Petrescu would know the position of every battalion, and likely could also decipher their future movements based on the types of supplies and their delivery locations. He certainly has access to sensitive and valuable information, and obviously someone up the chain thinks he also has motive to betray the Empire.

By the time I finish absorbing the dossier's information, the train has left Tanev and rocks gently westward. I turn out the small reading lamp and watch the occasional light slide by in the blackness outside my window. I'm amazed how dark the nights can be when the moon is gone, and there is no snow to reflect the starlight.

At some point I doze off with Petrescu's dossier still on my lap. Sloppy of me, I realize when I startle awake, disoriented and cold. Fuzzyheaded, I fumble my watch from my pocket. We should arrive in Kovrov soon, but outside the window it is still pitch black, with dawn still a few hours away.

Kovrov is nestled at the foot of a mountain pass that leads into the Empire's Romani Province. Before the current conflict, Korov was a thriving center for trade with the Papalate and other nations farther west. Goods came through the pass, down into Kovrov, then dispersed throughout the Empire on dozens of rail routes that radiated from the city like spokes on a wheel. The town's prosperity left with the trade, however, and while I have never been to Kovrov personally, I've read of its decline and decay—a golden fruit neglected to rot on a table in the sun. No wonder rumors of dissent are frequent from this region.

Shackles of Doubt

The train clatters as it changes tracks and makes a sharp turn north. We cross a river, a starlit line of falling riffles, and come into Kovrov proper. I can barely make out the dark buildings—squat blocks of gray and charcoal black fade into the night like a blur.

The train whooshes into a tunnel. The change in air pressure pushes painfully on my eardrums for a moment before everything equalizes. Brakes squeal and the deceleration tugs on me.

The platform comes into view, softly lit by hooded lamps spaced at regular intervals. After the darkness of the countryside, the train station looks like it's been lit with spotlights. I slide the dossier back into its envelope and stuff it into an interior pocket of my suit coat. I'll destroy it later, when I have better opportunity.

Even inside the station, the air is bitter cold, and I button my long coat up to my neck and push my hands into the pockets. Dozens of rail lines come into the station, but only a few platforms are lit. I follow the signs to my connecting train. Many of the soldiers move with me to the Coruşu-bound train on the far platform, and I linger to allow them to catch up and surround me. The company provides cover, if anyone were to be watching, which I think is unlikely, but why squander the opportunity for extra caution?

Waiting for us at the platform are tandem locomotives hauling three dozen armored flat cars and another dozen passenger coaches. The conductor checks my ticket at the platform gate then directs me to one of the two compartment coaches, the rest of the carriages being saloon cars. Once aboard, I stop at the toilet to burn Petrescu's dossier. I wash the soot from my hands and retire to my compartment, locking the door and pulling the shade so no one can see in from corridor. Hard bench seats line the opposite walls with luggage netting above them. Someone has carelessly left his hat in one of the nets. I leave the compartment's lamp dark, and sit so I can see out window. With the lights out, it will be difficult for anyone on the platform to see me.

The soldiers mill around in the cold, reluctant to board. Most wear the winter white and grays of the enlistments, a smattering of officer cuffs among them. Then something different catches my eye and pulls me up straight in my seat. The crowd parts and shifts away from two uniforms as they come slowly down the platform. Dark uniforms—nearly black—edged with gold epaulets and red cuffs, black *pilotkas* perched on their heads.

As they grow closer, my breath leaves me like I've been punched in the gut. It comes out as a hiss of air that forms into a name I hate: "Krauss."

The last time I saw Krauss he had Lera and me thrown off a train and stranded in the Empire's Central Mountains. That was one of my more pleasant encounters with him, too. What is he doing here? If I were a more paranoid person, I would assume he was following me, but he can't know of my presence on this train. He simply can't, yet here he is, passing my window, a smug expression of superiority on his face as the crowd parts before him in fear.

I shift around so I can watch him continue down the platform. Several cars down he boards.

Could my shadow from Tanev be behind this? I'm confident I wasn't followed from my meeting with R to the train station. Certainly my shadow has not yet even realized that I have given him the slip. When he does, he'll have no idea where I could have gone or how, so this must be coincidence. Yet coincidence like this leaves a pit in my stomach.

I take a sharp breath, realizing I haven't been breathing.

It's coincidence. No other explanation makes sense. There are only a few routes to the Romani front, so why should I be surprised to see a Red Cuff on the train? If it had been any Red Cuff other than Krauss, I would barely have noticed. But it *is* Krauss. And Krauss is always dangerous. Ever since El Emir, he's had a personal vendetta against me.

I get my breathing under control. I have the advantage this time because I know exactly where he is.

The train whistle sounds and the conductor yells the all-aboard. The milling soldiers pile into the coaches, creating a commotion in the corridor that lasts well after the train has pulled away from the station. The soldiers talk and sing and pass around bottles of vodka and wine. Cigarette smoke tickles my nose. Who can begrudge them a last bit of fun before returning to the trenches and the mud?

When the sun finally peeks over the horizon, we are climbing steadily upward into the mountains. Out my window, a solid forest of firs stretches up the slope, broken only by occasional limestone outcrops that shine stark white against the firs' almost black needles. Trees cling to the top of the outcrops and every slope that isn't sheer.

Cold air streams under my compartment door, and it sounds like a gale is ripping through the corridor. The soldiers raise a loud "Hurrah!" and based on the chatter, a vendor has arrived in the coach.

My stomach growls. I peer behind the shade into the corridor. A sea of bodies is packed in the narrow space like tinned mackerel. Craning my neck, I see a woman in a tight corset at the end of the coach. She has a tray perched on her hip with a strap with runs around her neck to hold it upright like a portable counter. In the tray are a dozen rows of tightly rolled *blini*. My mouth waters as she distributes the golden cakes with one hand while taking coins with the other. Slowly she moves down the smoky corridor toward me, her tray growing lighter with each step. As she reaches my compartment, I open the door, startling her.

I buy two cheese *blini* and retreat into my compartment to eat. The food makes me drowsy, but with Krauss so close, I don't want to sleep, so I brave the corridor for a second time and push my way forward to the end door and step outside. Cold wind rushes through my hair and immediately rouses me. The train clatters and rocks as we speed along the edge of a ravine filled at the bottom with a silver thread of a tumbling mountain stream. At this elevation, the fir trees are dusted with snow.

Standing in the crisp air, I realize how polluted with smoke the coach has become. I cough congestion out of my lungs. The incoming air, cold and dry, stabs painfully into my chest.

A shiver runs up my spine, but not the shiver of cold. The trees that, only a moment before, were rushing by seem to freeze for a second. My hair falls flat as the wind stops. Reeling, I catch myself on the chain railing to stop from tumbling down between the two carriages. As I do so the, the leather cord intended for my throat hooks on my chin.

I snap my left hand up to my throat to protect it from the garrote. My body wrenches back as my assailant forces a knee into my lower back for leverage and pulls. My feet scramble for balance, and I resist the instinct to use both my hands to right myself. I keep the one at my throat, ready to protect it then flail with my right, driving my elbow behind me. But in my current position, my blow glances harmlessly off my attacker.

I reach instead for my FP under my suit coat, but as my fingers graze the handle, my attacker twirls, spinning me around and off-balanced before driving me toward the railing. The chain pulls taut across my hips, and I'm nearly tossed over, but instead I lose my footing on an icy spot on the deck. The cord cuts into my chin as my full weight falls onto it, then it snaps up the side of my head, tearing my ear lobe. It would have ripped my nose off if I hadn't turned my head at the last moment. I crash to the deck, banging my tailbone on the metal. Flecks of dazzling light explode across my vision, and the train whistle that rips through the air drowns out my scream.

The world goes dark with a whump as the train plunges into a tunnel. The clacking of the wheels echoes off the tunnel walls and drums against my damaged ear.

I drop flat on the deck, tuck my arms, and roll away from the edge with as much force as I can generate. Then I strike my attacker's legs and he tumbles over me, bending awkwardly as his upper body catches on the chain railing. He folds past it and hits the deck next to me. I scramble to my feet, ignoring the throbbing pain in my ear.

My attacker, however, is quick and agile, and

somehow he's on his feet before I can get to mine. As I'm getting my footing, he wraps his arms around my torso, pinning my arms at my side. I try to break the hold, but he's too strong for me. With a grunt, he lifts my feet from the deck and starts to spin me toward the chain again. He's going to throw me over, and even if the train wheels don't slice me in half, I'll never survive the fall into the tunnel's rough stones.

As my feet come up and start to swing, I stab my toes at the only purchase I see: the latch on the coach's door. My foot catches under it and wrenches my body to a stop. The sudden jerk catches my attacker by surprise, and I slip free from his grip, falling hard once again to the deck, where I strike my head on the metal.

We barrel out of the tunnel then, the air pressure changing suddenly again and sucking my attacker forward. His feet catch a patch of ice, throwing him off balance as the train clatters over an even stretch of rails. His arms pin-wheeling, he falls heavily into the chain barrier.

I swing my feet around, my body spinning like a top, and strike his legs. They fly out under the chain and he tumbles off the platform. Desperately—and I don't know how he manages it—he grabs the chain with his left hand. The tendons in his wrist snap tight, his arm vibrates as his feet drag across the wooden ties racing by under the carriage.

I lunge for his arm, and grab his wrist as his hand rips free of the chain. I arrest his fall for a second, but he slides free of my grip then disappears under the carriage.

I squeeze my eyes shut, but the noise of the train is too great to hear his scream, if he does scream. The weight of the car and the sharpness of wheels would be enough to easily cut through any part of him that crossed the track. There's no possible way he could have survived.

"You're an idiot," I mumble at myself. I dropped my guard for a moment, and would have paid for it with my life if not for my Talent.

My ear throbs to the thumping of my heart. My hand comes away sticky, but my ear is still there, just cut along the bottom of the lobe as best I can tell. It probably looks worse than it is, and hurts more than it should.

Once I get to my feet I cautiously peer over the chain railing. No one is clinging to the coupling or hanging onto the undercarriage. Looking around the platform, I see no place he could have been hiding. The compartment door never opened. My gaze slowly rises. He must have come off the roof of the coach. Was he there when the train left the station, just waiting for me to come out? More likely he had been in among the soldiers, waiting for his opportunity, and when he saw me come out the front of the coach, he went out the opposite side and climbed up onto the roof. Looking now, I see how easy that would have been for someone with the nerve.

I look through the window into the coach and see only soldiers drinking vodka and singing. None of them seems to pay any attention in my direction. Was my attacker alone? Carefully I pull myself up so I can peer back along the carriage roof, but that, too, is empty of any threat. For the moment, at least, I am safe.

So who was he?

Red Cuff? Krauss did have someone with him, and

I'm forced to admit I was so focused on Krauss I never got a look at his comrade. I can't summarily dismiss the possibility, but this type of attack isn't their style. My attacker was a large man, too, and I while I do not recall Krauss's companion, I am fairly certain he wasn't a large man. Also, Krauss would have come at me with everything at his disposal, not sent a lone assassin to do what he would rather do himself.

As has become the case these past few weeks, I have only two other options to consider, and one of them doesn't make much sense, leaving me to suspect the enigma that is the Silver Tigers. They certainly embrace assassination as a tool; I've encountered several of their assassins before and found them extremely capable and dangerous. But like the Red Cuffs, how could he know I was on this train? It doesn't add up.

The cold begins to eat at me more than my uncertainty, so I cautiously return to my compartment and lock the door behind me. When I dab at my ear with the paper that held my *blini*, it comes away red. The reading light creates a glare on the window glass in which I can see myself. As I feared, the bottom of the lobe is torn and jagged, but it's not nearly as bad as I had thought, although much bloodier. My shirt collar is stained red, and splatters trail down the front. The wound needs stitching, but I don't have that luxury. I press the paper to it. If I can get the bleeding stopped, my long jacket will hide my shirt.

A short time later, we drop down the opposite side of the pass onto the central Romani plateau. It's full morning now, but the high plateau is surrounded by mountains and filled with cloud and fine falling snow that sticks to the window. Not that I could see much anyway, because as we arrive on the plateau, the tall firs and dark-needled pines close in on the track, solid as a prison wall. They grow close enough to the rail line that branches scrap across my window as we speed past.

The pain in my ear subsides to a dull throb, and carefully I lower the bloody paper. The wound has grown crusty, but the blood continues to ooze. The injury must look horrific.

The noise from the corridor has grown quieter; individual voices are now distinct where previously there was only a constant buzz, like a hive of ground-nesting hornets. Perhaps many of them have retired to their compartments to catch a last bit of peaceful sleep. Transport trucks will most likely be waiting at the station to take them down to the front. I try not to think about the young men, but it's hard not to wonder how many of them will never come back over these mountains.

Then, just before noon, the trees step back from the tracks, and we break onto open land that, during the summer, must be golden with wheat. We clatter past orchards and over streams, some frozen and snow covered, but others still running vigorously in the cold. Buildings become more frequent and change from rustic farm houses to large shops and residential neighborhoods. The Oka slides up next to our rail and we run parallel to its icy course. Ice rimes the edges of the swiftly running river.

We turn sharply and cross a metal truss bridge to come into Coruşu proper.

Coruşu is an old city of stone churches, noble manors, and cramped stone buildings jumbled together with seemingly little organization. Snow-crusted, cobblestone roads drift off in every direction, crossing at odd angles, looping back on themselves like a tangle of barbed wire. They narrow and widen when buildings unexpectedly come out of alignment, making them no place for modern autos. At the center of the city, rising above the squat buildings, is a low granite knoll topped with a large mansion of imposing gray stone. Round turrets cap each of the building's four corners. Three are squat, not even reaching above the steepled roof, but the last reaches upward several stories above every other building—an ancestral estate of Catherine Petrescu's family.

Prior to the Romani annexation into the Empire a century and a half ago, Coruşu had been the center of trade and governance on the central plateau. Prior to that, it had been fiercely independent, but, caught between the Empire and the Papalate, it was not large enough to fend off either. In the decades that followed its annexation, and under the Petrescu lineage, Coruşu became a functioning and important Imperial province.

We pull into the Coruşu train station, a long barnlike building with a curving roof where bare metal girders crisscross overhead. Many appear to be hasty additions, likely to shore up the structure, and a hole in the roof has been patched with steel plating. Steaming locomotives, either offloading or taking on supplies or troops, occupy every platform. Crates and sacks, casks and buckets, and bundles of tools and firewood are stacked nearly to the ceiling on pallets. Buzzing cranes and flywheel fork loaders shift the pallets around.

We shudder to a stop at a platform that lacks

palleted supplies and heavy loading equipment. These have been replaced with soldiers in winter white and grays wielding flechette rifles with bayonets. Men and women begin disembarking, but the corridor outside my compartment is eerily quiet, except for the shuffling of duffle bags and the scuffling of boots.

I wait for the soldiers to clear the coach before rising. My ear still throbs, but at least the bleeding has stopped, and I pull on my long jacket and button it to the collar to hide the blood on my shirt. I'll have to trust that no one notices the damage to my ear or the blood in my hair.

As I look at my reflection in the window, I notice again the hat in the luggage netting behind me. It's a worn fedora whose brim has gone floppy. It doesn't match my coat, but it'll work. I pull it onto my head, giving it a rakish tilt to better hide my damaged ear.

By the time I get onto the platform, many of the soldiers have filed away. A few of the armed ones linger, smoking cigarettes, but otherwise appear derelict in their guard duties. Anyone could get off this train now, and no one would notice.

No one seems to be watching the platform. I also see no signs of Krauss or his companion. They must still be on the train.

I walk with authority, as if I know exactly where I'm going. As I pass the guards, I nod curtly in their direction, and one of them raises his cigarette toward me and smiles.

The windows in the main lobby have been painted black—or maybe boarded up—and the interior lights are dimmed to the faintness of twilight. The voices of hundreds of soldiers echo through the high-ceilinged chamber, punctuated by the rapid clatter of train arrival and departure information cycling across the central clapperboard. Trains come and go, seemingly every second, and the flow of the information, the volume of soldiers and goods packed into this dim, cavernous space draws my gaze around the station as I cross toward the exit. Several moments pass before I notice a gaunt man in a short coat has fallen into stride at my side. His hair is a fuzz over a knobby head, and his eyes are sunken deep into pits in his face. If he hadn't been walking so energetically to keep up with me, I might have thought him seriously ill.

"You look tired, comrade. Perhaps I can recommend a guesthouse?"

This must be Mélon; he's fishing for the code phrase. I've never met Mélon, but that's not unusual. The Order is carefully structured into cells, and members of one cell seldom ever see those from another.

"No, just hungry," I say. "Where can I get a decent borscht?"

The fuzzy head shakes. "No, no," he says, almost chiding me. "You must try the *sarmale* at the Hanul cu Tei."

"Mélon?"

He nods.

"You have much to tell, or so a mutual friend has told me."

He points in a different direction than we are currently walking. "Out the east door to Ulita Mare. I know a quiet place we can talk."

"Lead the way."

Outside the doors we turn right on the Ulita Mare, a narrow road packed with troops and transport trucks. From the roof of one of the trucks an officer directs soldiers with a megaphone, but by all appearances he's failing; only a few soldiers have climbed into the back of the two dozen half-tracked vehicles. We hug the building wall. The stonework is soot-blackened, but heavily chipped, revealing gray stone beneath.

At the end of the building, Mélon turns right on the crossroad, and the uneven cobble street slopes down toward the Oka River. The road ends at a heavily treed park running along its bank. A gravel trail continues to the river's edge before turning downstream. Mélon directs me onward with a nod.

I hesitate. The trail is isolated and empty and gives me an uneasy feeling. The brush is thick enough to give cover to an assassin, but too sparse on the city side to obscure us from a shooter on the roof of a nearby building.

"It's safe." Mélon waits a few steps ahead of me on the path.

Other than professional unease, I sense nothing else. I'm not in any immediate danger, and other than general wariness, I have no reason to distrust Mélon. But I do not lower my guard. I fall in behind him as he leads the way down to the river trail.

The Oka River gurgles as it tumbles over stones, and chunks of ice outpace us in the swift, dark currents. We walk another two minutes in silence. By that time, the cold has gnawed my cheeks raw, and I long for the warmth of the station.

The trail passes under the stone arch of a bridge, and there Mélon stops us. He lights a hand-rolled cigarette, dragging on it several times before offering it to me.

I wave it aside.

He eyes me suspiciously as he spits a fleck of tobacco into the snow. "Tonight there will be an auction at the Guildhall," he says. "For the past year and a half, Petrescu has sponsored these monthly auctions, and we believe that's how he receives his communiqués. His auctions have become a significant event in an otherwise dreary social landscape, and the most powerful people in Coruşu, and some of the most influential in all of Romani, attend. Add to this that half of the proceeds go to assist families of those killed on the Westari front, and you can appreciate our need to proceed with caution. With no concrete evidence of guilt against Petrescu, it is, shall we say, politically inadvisable to disrupt a potentially legitimate auction. The ramifications would be far reaching and unpleasant."

Mélon pauses as a caravan of military trucks rumbles overhead.

My ear starts to throb again, but more from the cold than from the injury, I think. I don't like that my hands are buried deep in my coat pocket to protect them from the wind that funnels under the bridge. The gravel crunches under my shoes as I walk in place, trying to stay warm.

Mélon doesn't move, and after another minute, the military trucks have moved on and he lowers his gaze back to me.

"The auctions are handled by Goethel's."

My eyebrow rises. I know little about auctions, but everyone has heard of Goethel's. They are the world's premier auction house and deal in the most famous, most exceptional, and most expensive pieces of art and history. They are also based in Walzberg, putting them beyond direct control of the Empire.

"With the lack of evidence, we cannot get access to the items prior to the auction without Petrescu learning about our interest in him. We don't even know what will be placed up for bid tonight. No one does, which only heightens the interest and the bidding. Petrescu always buys at least one item. It's inside this item we believe the traitorous communiqué is hidden.

"You will outbid Petrescu on whatever he wants and return the artifact to me for examination. If the item is what we think, and we will find out once it is in our hands, we are confident Petrescu will seek to obtain it from you, providing more evidence of his treachery. You will sell it back to him, and the trap will close."

The plan seems elaborate—many points where things could wrong—but given our quarry, it is likely the best option we have. And it won't be easy to pull off. Petrescu is a man who wears success like a well-tailored shirt. Winning the auction against him will be difficult and expensive. Very expensive. He likely knows everyone in this part of the Empire with that kind of wealth, which must explain my selection for this task. My dark complexion and robust features don't exactly put me at home in Romani or any of the western provinces.

Mélon hands me a small envelope. Inside are a door key and a calling card.

"You have a room at the Petresi. Number four. You will find what you need there. The card—don't lose it. It is your pass into tonight's auction and cannot be replaced."

I tuck the envelope into my pocket. "Anyone else

of consequence operating here?"

"None of ours, as best I know."

"Papalate?"

Mélon shrugs. "We're very close to the front, so who can say with certainty. Unless you include Petrescu. Allegedly." He grins, his front teeth tobacco-stained.

"Red Cuffs?"

"The usual, but they've not been a problem. Of course, they know nothing about this operation, and it should stay that way."

"What about local insurgents?"

Mélon shakes his head—a crisp, dismissive motion. "Loyalty isn't a problem here. They know what would happen to them if the Papalate wins."

I want to press him about the Silver Tigers, but the certainty in his response suggest that if present they are still in hiding, and I'm hesitant to open myself to many questions. I thank Mélon for the information, and before we part ways, he gives me directions to the Petresi.

I continue along the gravel trail for another ten minutes until I come to a small waterfall where the river plunges into a ten-meter deep gorge. The path divides here, the western fork continuing along the lip of the gorge. I take the other, climbing a gentle zigzag up to a row of old buildings, and come out onto a narrow, stone street. It takes me a few seconds to get my bearings; then I head to the guesthouse.

今

THE PETRESI IS AN OLD STONE, two-floor building, with uneven walls and windows that aren't square. Planter boxes hang below the frosted panes, and I imagine they overflow with bursts of colorful flowers during spring and summer, but today they display only a blanket of snow and a latticework of ice. Icicles cling to the under eaves, except where a conscientious person has knocked them away above the entry.

The main sitting room is cozy, but I pass through it quickly, afraid that if I linger I'll attract the proprietor. My room is one of two up a narrow flight of worn, creaky stairs. My key sticks in the lock, but with a little force, it turns with a satisfying clunk. The room is small but decorated with antique furniture, the most impressive of which is a four-poster bed of darkly lacquered wood that takes up half the floor. On a small round table just inside the door, a folded piece of paper stands upright against a bottle of wine flanked by two glasses. From the texture, the card is homemade paper. The handwriting inside is delicate and beautiful. "Dear Mr. Tolnovski, we wish you a delightful stay in our home. If there is anything we can do make your stay more pleasant, simply ask. With regards, Mr. Andrei and Iulia Radu, Proprietors."

I set the card back on the table. I assume it's a nice a bottle of wine, although I probably could not tell the difference. I've always preferred vodka.

On the bed is a small cloth duffle. Laid out next a well-tailored long coat so as not to wrinkle are a black morning coat with gold buttons, a richly embroidered vest, white shirt, and black slacks. It's an impressive suit cut from fine wool and lined with silk. Inside the duffle I find a gold pocket watch engraved with the initials DT, socks, belt, gold cuff links that match the coat buttons, a handkerchief, shoe polish, assorted toiletries and a leather billfold. Inside the billfold is a sizable sum of money. In fact, I've never seen so much money before. It's likely more than I could ever dream to earn in a lifetime, and it sits heavily in my hand.

Unsettled, I drop the billfold back into the duffle.

Finally, I find another envelope tucked down at the bottom of the bag. In the envelope is a dossier on Dimitri Tolnovski, my cover.

I settle into the wingback chair by the window and read it in the gray winter light. The information is broad and lacks detail, but that's no surprise. The best aliases are ones that strike close to who I am because keeping track of details is easier—answer honestly when talking about unimportant things and fabricate only when necessary. A few falsehoods are easily tracked, and if skillfully applied, will muddle the truth if the ruse is ever detected.

According to the dossier, Dimitri Tolnovski owns

several iron mines in the far eastern province of the Empire. The mines were ceded to his family thirty years ago after being seized from the Quin in a minor border dispute. At the time, they were relatively unproductive, or they would have been given to a more prominent family of the Empire, but two decades later, large iron deposits were discovered, leading to Tolnovski's considerable wealth. Eight days ago, he traveled to Aurestapol on business and, upon hearing about the auction at a social function, requested an invitation.

I pull the calling card Mélon gave me from my coat pocket. The edges shimmer with gold leaf. Printed in raised black ink is Petrescu's family crest—a stylized raptor, wings spread, with crossed wheat stalks behind it. It's a powerful emblem, befitting of the Petrescu family history, which through ancient marriages, transcends the boundaries of Romani, Magya, and the Empire. Catherine, Petrescu's wife, was born in Romani—the Coruşu manor was a wedding gift to the couple from her father. Many members of the family still reside on ancestral lands spread across the vast western plain that spills out of the Empire's borders into neighboring nation states.

I set the card aside and study the information on Tolnovski until I grow drowsy and eventually nod off.

今

I AWAKE WITH A START to a dark room, and I'm
afraid for a moment that I have slept deep into the
night, but checking my watch, I find that I have an
hour until the auction starts. It's winter on the
Romani plateau, I remind myself; the days end early,
especially ones with cloud pack.

I lean close to the window and watch fat
snowflakes tumble by. The street below is dark and
only a few faint squares of light can be seen in the
otherwise shrouded city.

I pull the heavy curtains together before lighting a
small desk lamp. It casts just enough light to dress by.
It takes me several tries to get the cuff links secured,
and twice that to get an even knot in the tie, but
finally, after what seems an interminable amount of
time, I am ready.

I strap on my holster and adjust it so it won't show
under the heavy suit coat then set my pocket watch
atop my folded clothes and battered long coat on the
bureau. From this moment, I am no longer Calypto; I
am Dimitri Tolnovski. My back straightens. My

shoulder blades pull closer together, bringing my chest forward. Tolnovski is a made man, and he's confident. I check the gold pocket watch—*my* watch—and it's time to go.

At the bottom of the stairs, a middle-aged man and his wife meet me.

"Mr. Tolnovski," the man says, bowing slightly toward me. "Your auto has just arrived." He hurries before me and opens the door to the street. Outside, an auto hums at curbside. A man in a white shirt holds open the passenger door for me. Faint light spills out from the auto's interior, illuminating the snowy walk.

I pause in the doorway. Tolnovski would not forgo his manners. "You're Andrei Radu?" I ask, trying out an accent I once heard in Olvergraad in the Far East.

"I am." The man bows to me again; the hair on the top of his head is thinning.

"You have a lovely place, Mr. Radu. I doubt there is a finer room in all of Coruşu."

Radu looks up at me while he holds his bow. He is both surprised and pleased by my compliment. "You … are too kind, sir."

I move slowly and deliberately down the steps then duck into the waiting auto. The driver closes the door and comes around to the wheel. Without a word, he puts the auto into gear. The flywheel whirrs and we roll forward into the collecting snow.

The last time I had driven in snow like this was in Stephensberg when Lera and I were fleeing a Silver Tiger assassin. We barely escaped with our lives. That seems a long time ago now, but it was barely two weeks ago.

I wonder what Lera is doing at this moment, but

then regret it. Right now I shouldn't be thinking about her or anyone, for that matter, but I can't stop myself wondering how she is holding up to the rigorous training every new recruit receives. My first month training was physically brutal and emotionally harrowing. I don't know how that scrawny, scared kid from the state orphanage ever made it through. Yet here I sit in a fancy suit with a pistol strapped under my arm, heading to an auction of fine art to catch a traitor.

The training dismantled who I was, and rebuilt me into what I am now. Over the years, I have asked myself several times if it was worth it, and have never been able to settle on a consistent answer. Which makes me worry even more for Lera. She acts tough and smart, but the toughness is a façade. Who will she be when they are finished reshaping her?

The auto rolls to a stop. The driver climbs out and hustles around the front of the vehicle. I withdraw my hand from the door release. I almost forgot who I am; I need to focus.

The door opens, and I step out onto the dark street. In front of me, a shadowy building rises behind a stone wall topped with iron grillwork. A short walkway leads up to wide stone steps and stout wooden doors that shed faint light whenever they open. The outline of the Guildhall makes it appear a simple square structure, although imposing in size.

The vehicle pulls away, startling me.

Two couples, dressed as formally as I, go past me and up the steps. I follow, hesitant at first, but then catch myself and stride forward with confidence.

The wooden doors lead into a crowded vestibule where I check my long coat with an attendant. I'm motioned toward a second set of doors flanked by attendants wearing top hats and white gloves. After a quick inspection of my calling card, they wave me through.

I slip through a slit in the heavy blackout curtain and into the brightly lit chamber. Thick wooden columns support a balcony around the perimeter of a vast room before rising higher to an elaborately buttressed ceiling. Large iron chandeliers dangle by heavy chains from crossbeams as thick as the auto that brought me here. They spill warm yellow light across burgundy carpets deep enough to muffle the sound of the crowd that mills around in the open space between me and a dozen rows of chairs that fill the opposite side of the hall.

A couple jostles past me, and I realize I'm blocking the entrance and step farther into the room. With the crowd, the room is warm, and the noise is just loud enough to be inviting without being overwhelming.

"Your first time?" a woman asks me.

She has come up next to me holding a goblet of what I assume is red wine near her lips. The light reflecting off it gives her pale face a ruddy glow. Her dark hair is swept atop her head into an intricate knot before the ends cascade down her back. The knot is held in place with a netting of stones that shimmer in the light. She has delicate features and a slender chin that pulls down into a point, giving her face the appearance of an inverted teardrop. Rich brown eyes appraise me.

"Is it that obvious?" I ask.

She sips her drink. "No, just a conversation starter."

I can't place her accent, but she's not from the

Empire. Perhaps a diplomat's wife, yet her hand holding her drink is curiously bare of ornamentation. In fact, other than the gems in her hair, she wears no jewelry, which is peculiar, given the amount of finery in the room.

"I'm Katalin Kovac." She extends her hand.

I take it, not sure if I'm supposed to kiss the fingers. I chose to incline my head toward to her. "Dimitri Tolnovski."

"I've not seen you before, and I never forget a face, Mr. Teneski."

"Tolnovski," I correct gently, "and that may be because I have never been to one of these before."

"A startling oversight," she says, sipping from her goblet. "What is your business in Coruşu? Oh, come, do not look surprised. I am no spy." She grins mischievously. "It's just that no one comes to Coruşu anymore for pleasure, what with the war."

"But it is pleasure."

A waiter with a tray of drinks slows as he goes by us. I take what looks like a snifter of brandy, but one sip and I realize it's something different, but not unpleasant.

"I came in from Aurestapol today," I say, "specifically for the auction. I have no other business here."

"So you are an art lover, then?"

"Not really." I know nothing about art, but I suspect she does, and therefore any conversation down that road could be treacherous. "I simply admire beautiful things."

Her lips part a little into a vague smile. Her eyes sparkle in the room's warm light.

I suddenly feel hot. "I would also guess that

Coruşu is not your ancestral home."

"Very perceptive, Mr. Tol ..."

"Tolnovksi." I say.

"Tolnovski, yes." Her hand brushes my arm, and I force myself to hold my position and not to step back from her. My senses aren't tingling, but something about her forwardness puts me on my guard.

"I am not a citizen of your fine Empire," she says. "I come from a little place called Szarvos. Perhaps you have heard of it?"

Szarvos is the largest city in Magya State, the Empire's western neighbor, with whom we have had a long an on-again, off-again relationship. Currently the two countries are on friendly terms, but rumors of shifting alliances are common, and most in the Empire expect Magya State to realign with the Papalate before all this is over. I've been to Szarvos once before, but didn't see much of the city and had to leave in a hurry.

"I've been to a few of these affairs," Katalin continues, "but nothing has ever caught my fancy enough to get me to bid. But who knows, looking around, I've already seen one thing that interests me." She places her now-empty glass on a passing tray and takes another. "Would you care to join me while I look around?" She extends her arm to me.

I crook my elbow and she loops her arm through it. She guides me gently toward a row of display tables along the left side of the hall that, due to the crowd in front of them, I failed to notice when I entered. Heads turn as we pass. We must make an unorthodox pairing: her petite, pale frame in a red satin dress contrasting my dark suit and complexion. Her head barely comes to my shoulder, but she demands attention, and she gets it.

As we approach the first table, the people move aside, allowing us to examine the bronze statue that sits upon it. Evidenced by the halos around two of the figures, it appears to be a religious sculpture of some sort. A printed card sits next to it on the table giving details about the artwork: the artist, its dimension, materials, date of creation, and a brief description I don't bother to read. A man stands alertly behind the table; he wears white gloves and doesn't make eye contact with us. Stitched on his jacket is the emblem of Goethel's.

"A Balotelli," Katalin says, nodding at the bronze. "Too provincial for my tastes."

It's a nice piece, certainly; even I can see that, but it's one of dozens you might see in Auretapol's Royal Institute of Fine Art. All those endless paintings and sculptures run together in a generic blur for those not well versed in artistic nuance. I say nothing, and we move to the next table, on which sits a single small painting. It's a landscape of mountains and rolling green hills, unimpressive in my opinion except for its ornate golden frame. The card says it by a Romani painter.

"The brush work is impressive," Katalin says. "Meticulous, but bold."

I expect her to say something flirtatious, but she doesn't. Instead, we move on to the next table and the next, down to the end of the row. At each she offers some comment on the displayed piece, usually disparaging, but on occasion complimentary. None of the pieces seems to appeal to her enough that she would consider placing a bid on it. For the most part, I offer little conversation. The works are finely crafted, even I can see that, but I lack sufficient knowledge to truly appreciate any of them.

As we cross the room to the tables on the opposite side of the hall, I ask, "Do you know the Petrescus? I want to thank them for the invitation." I had been scanning the room, but had yet to locate them.

"I know of them," Katalin says, "but I've never been formally introduced."

"Can you tell me if you see them?"

She squeezes my arm. "Anything for you, Mr. Tolnovski."

Unlike the other tables, there is no crowd gathered around the open briefcase on the next one. The attendant stands behind it with his arms crossed and feet apart as if guarding a door at an exclusive club in Aurestapol. Inside the briefcase, nestled in a soft shell of cut foam, is an ornate sphere about the size of an ostrich egg. It's mottled black with faint patches of other color bleeding through the lacquer. A silver filigree, like an intricate lace, encompasses the entire object, gleaming sharply in the light.

I'm drawn closer, and leaning over it, I see the mottling is actually an array of small stars splashed across the black night. This close, the silver lacework dissolves into a series of intricate symbols, and a moment passes before I recognize them as letters and numbers in the Latin alphabet. The detail and intricacy are stunning.

I look at the card next to the case:

> Celestial Orb (circa 1720)
> Unknown artist
> Porcelain & silver

The origin and crafter of this exquisite artifact is unknown, but the glazes date to the early 18th century. The orb accurately portrays the night sky on the winter solstice at the latitude of the Emperor's great city, demonstrating the artist's detailed knowledge of astronomy. Six intricate rings, three rotating horizontally and three vertically, are inscribed with numbers (on five rings) and the months of the year (on one ring). The craftsmanship of the interlocking rings is a mystery and resembles nothing known elsewhere.

Most experts believe the orb is a calendar, but some postulate it is a complex puzzle box which, to date, has never been successfully opened. The true nature of the Celestial Orb is unknown.

"Exquisite, is it not?" says a male voice.

Startled, I snap upright, nearly spilling my glass of brandy-but-not-brandy. A couple has joined us at the table; they are leaning past me trying to get a closer look at the orb in its case. I step to the side to allow them a better view.

"Exquisite is an understatement," I say. "I've never seen anything like it."

The man is tall, with streaks of silver in his dark and wild hair. He props himself up with a straight cane, although he doesn't seem to be favoring either leg. His companion, who I assume is his wife, wears a dark blue gown with a high collar and long sleeves. The corset of the dress is intricately embroidered with silver thread and what look like small pearls.

"I'd like a closer look," the man says.

The attendant nods and lifts the orb from its case with his gloved hands. He rotates it slowly to reveal the underside of the orb. I lean closer for a better look, but I'm partially shielded by the couple.

"May I?" The man extends his hands.

"Certainly, Mr. Petrescu."

Petrescu?

The man takes the orb in his left hand and straightens, and for the first time I get a good look at his face. Arkady Petrescu in the flesh is thinner than the one I saw in the picture, and his hair is streaked with more gray than I imagined. Authority radiates from him, however; he is imposing both in height and presence.

"Would you hold this for a moment, Catherine?" Petrescu hands the orb to her.

His wife is beautiful, even at her age. The skin has loosened under her chin, but her face still glows with youth and vitality. Her eyes are keen. She turns the orb in her hands, experimentally rotating one of the rings a single position.

Petrescu tucks a monocle into his right eye then takes the orb back from his wife.

"It's beautiful," Catherine says. "It would be a perfect anniversary gift."

Petrescu makes a gentle noise, as if this is a conversation they have had before. He leans close to study the orb for a moment before carefully returning it to the man in the white gloves. Petrescu removes the monocle then tucks it into the pocket of his morning coat.

I feel guilty watching this intimate moment. When Catherine looks over at Katalin and me, my gaze drops to the floor.

"We will have been married forty years in exactly one week," she says.

"Coronation Day?" Katalin says in surprise.

"The same day, yes," Catherine says, "but some … few … years earlier."

"Has it been that short a time?" Petrescu asks.

Catherine tugs playfully at his ear, and Petrescu grins.

I resist the urge to touch my own ear. The wound still throbs.

"Every year has been better than the last," he says to her, before turning his attention suddenly to me. "I do not believe we've met. I am Arkady Petrescu."

We shake hands. His grip is firm, the motion short and authoritative.

"I am Dimitri Tolnovski." I nod as I speak so that I do not have to look into his eyes. "This is Miss Kovac. She is visiting from Szarvos." I motion across my body to Katalin, who has resumed her position on my arm, much to my surprise.

"My beautiful wife, Catherine," Petrescu says.

I bow to her. "The pleasure is mine."

"Tolnovski you say." Petrescu's brows pinch together, and I can almost hear the inner machinations turning as he tries to place the name. The tension in his forehead releases suddenly. "You're the gentleman from the east who came down from Aurestapol."

"I am. And I thank you for the opportunity to be

here tonight."

"I hope it lives up to your expectations."

"It already has, I assure you."

"Is this your first visit to Coruşu?" Catherine asks.

"It is my first to Romani," I say. "From what I've seen since I've arrived, Coruşu is a lovely city, especially considering how close it is to the front."

"The distance may be close as the raven flies," says Petrescu, "but there is an entire mountain range between us. Winter is no blessing, except in that it relieves us from any threat of invasion for a few months. Curse the beautiful and wonderful snow." He shakes a fist theatrically at the sky, and Catherine laughs.

"But I see that Mr. Tolnovski has discovered a little something to help him stay warm." She nods at my glass. "Vinars we call it. It's a bit of an acquired taste, sort of like a cognac but different."

"I'm enjoying it," I say, and realize it's the truth. Vinars is no vodka, but then nothing quite compares.

"What is it that brings you west, Mr. Tolnovski?" Catherine asks. "That is a great distance to travel, especially in these difficult times."

She does not go into details, and I wonder if she is referring to the time of the year or if she knows about the unrest in the Empire's middle provinces. For the most part, I have been impressed by how effectively the ministries have controlled the news. Few in Aurestapol even seem aware of the unrest elsewhere in the Empire. I wasn't fully aware of the depth of it until my last mission to Olesk, and more specifically St. Stephensberg, which was practically under military law.

"I had pressing business in Aurestapol," I say, as

nonchalantly as I can. "Under the Emperor's grace, I operate several iron and silver mines, but I don't want to bore you, so the less said about that, the better."

"And what brings you to Coruşu, Miss Kovac?" Catherine asks, turning to Katalin.

"I'm going south to visit a dear relative. I have attended a previous auction as a guest of the Moronovs, but we've never been formally introduced."

"Yuri has never been known for his etiquette." Catherine's eyes narrow, and I get the feeling she is appraising Katalin as she would a delinquent member of her household staff. Then, just as quickly, the lines radiating from the corners of her eyes smooth.

Katalin doesn't seem to notice, however, and the two women turn away from Petrescu and me to continue their conversation about Katalin's travels. Petrescu's intense gaze makes me feel suddenly exposed.

"Has anything here caught your eye, Dimitri?"

"I know nothing about art," I admit.

"Good art stirs the passion in your soul. That's all you need to know. Surely there is something here that does that?" He arches his brow mischievously.

"You sound like a salesman," I say with a smile to signal I mean no insult.

To my relief Petrescu laughs.

"All for a good cause. Half of the auction proceeds go toward a relief fund for the families of those killed in his dreadful, albeit necessary, conflict."

"I admire that. To answer your question, I've seen some things that appeal to me, but I don't wish to tip my hand to a rival bidder. You seem the type who would drive up a bid ... for the sake of charity."

"I might," he says, his voice level and serious sounding, but his eyes twinkle with mirth.

Petrescu takes his wife's arm and gently pulls her away from Katalin. "The bidding is about to start," he says. They head toward the chairs at the front of the hall—nearly all of them are taken—as the auctioneer steps onto a makeshift dais and waits patiently for the crowd to settle.

Katalin takes my arm again and leans in toward me. The faint yet not unpleasant smell of musk tickles my nose. "We should sit."

Yes, she's right. We should sit. Other than a handful of people still lingering around the tables of artifacts or gathered around the perimeter of the seating area, everyone has found a chair.

She leads me toward the aisle running down the middle of the chairs, breaking the rows into two sections, like pews in a cathedral. As we pass one of the attendants, he hands me a placard with the number forty-two on it. He makes no attempt to give one to Katalin, and she doesn't ask for one either. I wonder if she doesn't intend to bid on anything or if she's decided that I should buy something for her. The thought unnerves me, as much by how presumptuous such a maneuver would be from someone I've just met, as the fact that I know nothing about this woman except what she's told me. She could be anyone: an enemy spy, a Red Cuff, or even a Magya princess. But mostly I'm unnerved because I suddenly realize that until this moment, my guard has been dropped simply because she is a beautiful woman.

I steer us toward two empty seats near the back. Katalin pulls gently but insistently at my arm, wanting to be closer to the front. I almost acquiesce, but then realize if I sit up front, I won't be able to watch Petrescu, who sits only a row ahead on the opposite side of the aisle from the seats I've selected. When I don't budge, Katalin frowns, but she acquiesces, and we take our seat as the first item, a painting we did not have time to review, is brought to the front of the room.

I casually watch Petrescu, who follows the bidding intently. I've never been to an auction before, so I struggle to keep my attention on both Petrescu and the proceedings. The bidding progresses quickly at first, with multiple parties flashing their numbered placards, sometimes boldly, sometimes subtly, and the auctioneer somehow seeing them and acknowledging them. The bidders dwindle to just two then finally one, but before the item can be sold, a new person enters the fray and eventually wins the painting with a bid that exceeds what I make in a year. I try not to react to the amount; after all, it's a paltry sum to Tolnovski.

The Balotelli sculpture is up next and the bidding begins without Petrescu. I wonder if Petrescu is a bidder who engages early and tries to outlast the competition, or if he's the type who lets others do the pedestrian work before stepping in at the end to claim the prize. I try to remember what kind of officer he was. I know he was one of the Empire's most effective battlefield leaders, but I know little about his command style.

"The one with the beard wants this one," Katalin whispers. She nods toward a man with an impressive amount of facial hair who casually raises his placard, and whom the auctioneer acknowledges.

"Why do you say that?" I ask.

"A game I like to play, and I'm pretty good at it, too." She must see my expression of doubt because she pinches my arm playfully and says, "Just watch."

After several tense rounds, the sculpture goes to the bearded man. The audience applauds his generosity, and he rises and bows to the room, much to Katalin's delight.

I'm impressed, but I'm not about to admit it to her. "Lucky guess, I say."

The next item is the Celestial Orb.

"This one, Petrescu wants," she says, "but I don't think he's going to get it."

"Why do you say that?"

She grins at me enigmatically. In that moment, Petrescu raises his placard and the auctioneer acknowledges his opening bid. A second bid comes in, then a third from the opposite side of the aisle. My head swings around rapidly, following the auctioneer's pointing hand, but he's moving so quickly now that I never have time to focus on the identity of the bidder before a new bid comes and my head swings to locate the new person, as if my nose is attached to the auctioneer's hand by a string. Slightly dizzy, I rip my gaze away from the front of the room and send it back to Petrescu. The price has already tripled and Petrescu has not re-entered the bidding. I'm beginning to believe his opening offer was made merely to break his monotony. As quickly as I have that thought, I dismiss it. Petrescu is a man of action and, as best I can tell, everything he does is for a larger purpose.

Petrescu raises his placard a second time and seizes the lead. By this time, the number of bidders has dwindled, and they collectively hesitate. A tense second passes. The auctioneer tries to coax a higher amount from a couple near the front, but the woman shakes her head. Petrescu has bid a large sum, and my sensibilities seem to handcuff my arm from rising. Petrescu's bid would have kept my orphanage in food and clothes for three, maybe four, years. With all the shortages here and in Aurestapol, this entire affair is offensive, no matter what good it might be doing for the families of the war dead.

But I have a job, and if Petrescu is the man The Order thinks he is, then he bears responsibility for those war dead. Money spent saving lives is better than money spent placating those who have already lost their loved ones.

My hand raises the placard sheepishly, but the auctioneer doesn't immediately notice it. Katalin pushes my elbow and the placard comes up higher. The auctioneer points at "number forty-two, the gentleman in the back" and the eyes of the room rotate toward me. Sweat pimples my forehead and armpits. The room, which had been comfortably warm a moment ago is now sweltering. The noise of the crowd has disappeared, and the voice of the auctioneer has become distorted, as if we've all plunged into a clear lake. His finger continues to point toward me, and I flash back to my childhood when the other boys would point at me and laugh. I don't know why I remember that at this moment. I've stared down the barrel of a pistol and into a three-story drop from an icy building ledge, but the auctioneer's pointing finger gives me cold sweats worse than either of those.

After what feels like an eternity, the finger swings

away from me, and the sound of the room returns to normal as if the speed of a phonograph has been corrected. The focus of the room follows the auctioneer's hand. My eyes follow, too, across to Petrescu holding his placard aloft.

The stab of disappoint surprises me. I have never liked attention; attention has always meant pain, both physical and mental. I suppose it's one of the reasons I do what I do because if I am doing things right, I operate beneath the notice of my adversaries and my allies. I am most effective when I am unseen.

I raise my placard with authority this time because that is exactly what Tolnovski would do. He is used to the attention, and not shy about seizing what he wants, and I know now that he wants the Celestial Orb.

"The gentleman in the back," says the auctioneer, but my bid stands for only a second before Petrescu raises it. I don't hesitate to raise my placard again. To be honest, I don't know how much I've just bid. That's probably for the best, although concern that the envelope in my pocket might come up light nags at my mind.

Tense murmurs slide around the room. They are different from the excited comments that accompanied the other bids, and I wonder if I have done something inappropriate, but I shake off that feeling when Katalin squeezes my knee reassuringly. Tolnovski has done nothing wrong.

Petrescu stares at me as he raises the bid again. He appears mildly amused.

As quickly as the auctioneer's hand begins to slide away from me, I raise my placard and the pointing finger reverses course.

Shackles of Doubt

Petrescu's amusement dissolves into a pinched frown. His wife whispers into his ear, and he shakes his head curtly. I'm not sure if he's answering a question or expressing disagreement with her. Regardless, he doesn't look pleased when he raises his placard, this time in my direction.

I immediately follow suit. No hesitation, I decide. Make clear to Petrescu that I will not be denied.

The murmurs in the room have ceased and the hall is quiet, except for the drone of the auctioneer. The other bidders have bowed out, and the auctioneer has focused his attention on coaxing more money from Petrescu.

The muscles in my neck are tight; my body perches on the edge of the seat. The whole room sits there with me, too. All eyes are focused on Petrescu as he considers his next move. A few of those eyes dart back to me, but never for long because the show, right now, is Petrescu's. I get the impression few have ever challenged Petrescu during the past, and the crowd is both excited and appalled that the "gentleman in the back," whom they've never seen before, is challenging their benefactor.

As I assess the mood of the room, my eye catches on a figure standing against the wall. It takes my brain a second to register that something is familiar about her, and to bring my head back around. She is tall, nearly two meters in height, and her arms and shoulders, exposed by her simply cut dress, are lean muscle. Her face is angular, softened only by wisps of blond hair that dangle down from her crown braid.

And then it clicks, like I've been hit with a crowbar.

Dai Li.

The last time I saw her, we were fleeing from a café in Olesk where the Red Cuffs had gunned down two-dozen people while searching for someone named Valentin.

As those unpleasant memories flood in, Dai Li's eyes lock with mine, but unlike me, her recognition is immediate.

A tug on my arm pulls my attention away from her. Katalin's eyes are wide, and I realize then the entire room is looking at me.

"The gentleman in the back, do you wish to bid?"

Disoriented, I look at the placard in my hand then back at Dai Li, but she is no longer standing along the wall, but is walking toward the exit at the back of the hall. Petrescu studies me from across the aisle. The attendant at the front tilts the padded case with the Celestial Orb in my direction.

"Do you want to bid, sir?" the auctioneer asks.

Dai Li is nearly to the door.

I stand up, waving my placard. "I will triple Mr. Petrescu's bid."

The room erupts in noise and motion. The auctioneer acknowledges my bid and looks at Petrescu who shakes his head.

"Sold to the gentleman in—"

I push past Katalin, but I barely get to the aisle when I'm met by a crowd. Everyone in the room has risen to their feet and is applauding my generosity. They've flooded forward to take my hand and congratulate me, but begging their forgiveness, I push through their hands and bull my way forward until I'm free. Ahead, the blackout curtain swings back into position. I run out into the lobby, and then outside into the falling snow.

After being inside the brightly lit hall, I'm night blind. An auto door slams closed at the curbside, and I leap down the Guildhall steps, reaching the roadside as the auto pulls away.

"Stop!"

But the auto drives on, leaving me in the cold, falling snow, winded from my failure.

What is Dai Li doing in Coruşu? It can't be a coincidence that she's here the same time as I, but she couldn't be following me, unless my attacker on the train was working with her and got word of my travel off before his death. At this point, I guess anything is possible. But she is the key to so many of questions, and she just drove off into the night.

Before I can turn to go back into the Guildhall, I hear the unmistakable hiss of an FP pressurizing.

"Show me your hands or I will shoot you." It sounds like Katalin's voice, but the accent is gone. "Don't turn around." The tip of the pistol jabs sharply between my shoulder blades.

I raise my hands and stay where I am. A hand reaches up under my suit coat and removes my weapon. I smell musk.

"Who are you really?" I ask.

"I could ask you the same," says Katalin.

An auto slides to a stop next to me in the slush.

"Get in."

I climb into the dark back seat. Katalin slams the door on my heels and the locks click into place. She climbs into the front passenger seat and trains her FP back at me.

"Let's go," she says to the driver, and the vehicle rolls away into the night.

PART II

INTO THE FIRE

今

KATALIN THROWS me a cloth sack. "Put it on," she says with a wave of her FP. The hood isn't needed. It's so dark out that I can't see where we're going and don't know the streets of Coruşu well enough to figure it out from the turns of the car or the shadowy shapes of the buildings. But I do as I'm told, and settle back in the seat, my arms folded across my chest.

I should be afraid, but I'm more annoyed than anything. If Katalin wanted me dead, she wouldn't have bothered with the hood. I'm annoyed because I couldn't have made this easier for her. She possibly planned to accompany me after the auction and then make her move. I wouldn't have invited her to come, and her insistence would have raised my guard, making her task that much more difficult, and likely thwarting it all together. But I made it easy for her by rushing outside into the lonely dark. Seeing her opportunity, she made her move. Yes, annoyed is the right word for my current state.

She wants me alive, so now the question is "Why?"

Am I her prisoner, or has someone else hired her? If I'm her prisoner, then who is she? Does she know who I really am, or is this a kidnapping for money, and I turned out to be the unlucky mark? I've done nothing but foolishly demonstrate I'm incredibly wealthy and a good ransom target.

That seems too coincidental, but sometimes coincidence is exactly how the world works. It just feels wrong in this case. If it's not coincidence, then I was targeted, which means either Katalin or the person she works for, knows who I am, and what my alias would be tonight.

I think I can dismiss Dai Li as a suspect. The Papalate? What could the Papalate possibly want with me? I don't know anything of value about troop movements or military strategy. Unless they are onto my current mission and protecting Petrescu, but that would mean … no, I can't accept a traitor within The Order. Petrescu himself? I did just outbid him for the orb, but I can't see any connection between him and Katalin, given the recent exchange in the Guildhall. The Silver Tigers, then—other than Dai Li, at least? They've already shown considerable interest in me— or least in seeing me dead—and they seem to be more than just a pedestrian revolutionary group. I can't easily dismiss them, but they, too, don't feel right; they have always seemed more intent on killing me than capturing me. The Red Cuffs? Hmm, Krauss is a distinct possibility, especially considering he was on the train. But unless he, too, has an informant inside The Order, how could he know I was here posing as Tolnovski? The Red Cuffs aren't competent enough to infiltrate us.

Perhaps they have a Talent at their disposal? The

Order doesn't have monopoly on people like me. I try to recall everyone I've seen since leaving Tanev, but it's not like those of us with Talents have brands on our cheeks marking us for what we are. Even so, the thought of a Talent helping Krauss and his comrades is unsettling.

My brain is working too hard in the silence. This line of thinking isn't going to get me anywhere, and is ultimately counter-productive. At this moment, the allegiances of my captors are unimportant.

I don't expect an answer, but I ask, "Where are we going?"

As expected, Katalin doesn't respond. We drive on, the flywheel engine humming faintly. The tires of the auto crunch through the snow piling up in the street.

"If it's money you want, I can arrange that," I say, doing my best to stay in cover and fish for information at the same time.

"There," Katalin says, not to me, but the driver. The auto rolls to a stop. The back door opens, and I'm greeted by a blast of cold air and hands that drag me out of the seat.

"Make him comfortable," Katalin says. "I'll be back soon."

Doors slam, and the auto spins back up with a whir. With escorts on each side of me and a pistol point tucked under my ribs, I'm led through the dark. Snow and wind chill my fingers.

"Stairs," one of my escorts says, and I step up just in time to catch the first step. It's uneven with packed snow, but my two escorts make sure I don't fall. We pass out of the snow, and I assume I've come inside because the air, while still cold, is no longer frigid, and the wind is gone.

The hands never leave my arm. They guide me forward across what sounds and feels like a stone floor covered with grit or debris of some kind. We climb several wooden stairs, up to the next floor. The place doesn't get warmer as we go, and we take the steps carefully so I don't fall. We turn right and go straight for twenty-two more steps before we come to a stop.

"Make yourself comfortable," my escort on my right says. He yanks the hood from my head, and I'm pushed forward into a small room devoid of furnishings. They close the metal door; two bolts snap into place, casting me into darkness except for the thin line of light bleeding through the crack along the bottom. After the drive and the hood, my vision is already adjusted to the darkness, and that meager light is enough for me to see my cell. With my arms extended, I could almost touch the opposite walls, so maybe two meters wide by four long. The door is in the middle of the narrow wall. The ceiling is too high to touch, and in the center of it is driven a metal ring about the diameter of my fist. Next to the ring is a dark metal grate, through which cold air streams into the cell, making it as icy as a meat locker. The wall opposite the door is raw brick. Driven into it are two rows of four stout metal rings, slightly smaller than the one in the ceiling. The lower row is about waist height, while the upper row is at my eye level. The other walls are cracked plaster over stout wooden planks.

It's a secure room.

All I can do now is bide my time. I sit in one of the corners opposite the door and pull my knees up to my chest. My breath mists around my head, settling slowly in the still air. I tuck my fingers into my armpits to warm them. If I had my long coat it wouldn't be too bad. My wool suit coat is sufficient for now, but won't be if my stay is extended. Sitting on the stone-tiled floor will suck the warmth out of me if I'm not careful, but I cannot rest standing up, and I suspect I will need all my strength if I'm going to get out of here. I lean my head against the wall and let my eyes close. I am in no immediate danger, but I am certain that will not be the case later.

今

THE BOLTS SLIDING on my cell door jar me awake.
The door opens, throwing a blindingly bright
rectangle of light on the floor. I squint at the two
hulking shadows that advance and pull me to my feet.
My head still fuzzy with sleep, I allow them to lead
me into the corridor. I look to the left, in the
direction I was brought in from Katalin's car, but a
heavy curtain blocks the hallway. Directly across from
my cell is another door, but this one looks like new
construction based on the bare wood frame and the
door's utilitarian appearance that doesn't match the
corridor's otherwise elegant, albeit faded, wallpaper,
slightly worn carpet, and brass light sconces. These
are dark; the hallway's harsh light emanates from a
naked bulb dangling from a cable stapled to the
ceiling and down the wall to a lead-acid battery sitting
on the floor next to my cell door.

I'm turned away from the curtain, and nudged
down the remainder of the short hallway that ends at
a black-painted sheet of plywood, likely covering a
window. Stout wooden doors with ornate panels and

intricate brass handles are on opposite sides of the corridor. The two guards push me inside the one to my left, and quickly close it behind me.

This room is about the three times the size of my cell and has a table with a single chair. On the table is a glass of water and a plate with cheese, a few slices of bread, and some sausage links. Like the corridor, the room is harshly lit by a single bare bulb hanging from the middle of the ceiling by a wire hooked to a battery near the door. Plywood sheets have been nailed securely over the room's windows and the walls have been painted white. One of the walls is recent construction; I can tell because the wainscoting that lines the other three walls doesn't continue onto it, and the plastering is sloppy workmanship.

Someone has gone to some trouble to make this place, but didn't have the time or perhaps the inclination to do a good job of it.

At least we're starting to make progress.

I expect any moment I'm going to find out who is behind all this. In the meantime, I sandwich the cheese and sausage between the bread and shove it into my mouth.

The sandwich goes down easily. The water is cold, about the same temperature as the room, and has a slight metallic taste. As I set down the cup, the door opens and Katalin enters, but it's the person who follows her in that twists my gut and nearly makes me vomit up the food.

"I should have known," I say as Krauss positions the chair he's carrying on the opposite side of the table from the one already there.

"Sit down and shut up," Krauss says. "I'm in no mood for your games, Calypto."

The sharpness of his tones catches me off guard. Krauss generally prefers to needle with snide comments and calculated digs at my loyalty. I've only seen him lose his calm once before, in El Emir, and the thought of that gives me a shiver.

Seeing no advantage to antagonizing him, I sit down.

"When are you going to get it through your head that we're on the same side," I say to Krauss.

"When you start acting like it," he says. "But that isn't going to happen, now is it?"

"Let's all be nice," Katalin says. "This doesn't have to be hard."

Krauss's jaw clenches. The muscles on the side of his face stand out. If he squeezes any harder, his teeth might shatter.

Katalin sits in the chair opposite me. Gone are her fancy dress and the elegant hair. She wears a charcoal, knee-length skirt and a white blouse. Her hair is pulled back from her face and wound tightly into a bun on the top of her head. It's held in place with two metal sticks I suspect could double as weapons. She wears no makeup, but her skin is flawlessly smooth, like a doll's. She looks like a warden of a notorious prison, if a woman could be such a thing.

She sets a briefcase on the table. I recognize it immediately as the one from the auction last night.

"Is your name even Katalin?" I ask.

"My name is not important."

"Then why not tell me?"

"I'm asking the questions." Katalin's voice is cold and sharp. She is used to being in charge, and the order of things becomes clear. No wonder Krauss is biting his tongue.

"I'm—"

"I know who you are, and who you work for. I don't care. Traitors wear many shirts."

The directness of her accusation catches me off guard. I have little love of the Red Cuffs, but I also thought my problems with them were restricted to Krauss. He is far from harmless, but I never gained the impression he'd convinced anyone higher in his organization that I was a legitimate threat. If he had, I doubt I'd be sitting here now.

"I'm not a traitor," I say, but it comes out sounding weak.

"We shall see."

Krauss snaps the releases on the briefcase. The Celestial Orb nestles in the soft foam packing. Even in the room's stark light, it's beautiful enough to draw my breath away.

He slides the open case to me. "Open it."

I shake my head, not sure what he's asking me.

"Open it," Krauss says again.

"The orb?"

"Of course the orb."

"I can't."

"You can't or you won't?" His tone is filled with malice.

"I don't even know what this is," I say. I see no harm in telling them that; it's the truth. "I don't know how to open it."

Krauss sits on the edge of the table next to me and rolls up the sleeves of his white shirt to his elbows. The muscles in my shoulders and neck tighten, preparing to move if necessary, but there isn't any need. Krauss's actions reek of calculation, and this is a cheap interrogator's trick. He's going to threaten me, maybe even hit me, and Katalin is going to be the voice of reason that is supposed to win me over and make me want to help her. Krauss doesn't make a move toward me, however. He looms over me reeking of blood sausage.

"You know how this can go," he says, his voice restrained and barely audible in the silence of the room. The quietness of it curdles my stomach. "We did this once before, or at least we started it."

El Emir. Yes, he started it, but I finished it.

"This time I'll finish it," he says.

"Control yourself, Mr. Krauss."

And there it is, exactly as I expected it to play out. The Red Cuffs are predictable.

Krauss moves away from me. He taps two cigarettes from a pack he produces from the breast pocket of his shirt and lights them, blowing the blue-gray smoke up toward the bare bulb. The cheap tobacco's acrid stink attacks my nose and brings water to my eyes. He offers me one, but I wave it away. With a shrug, he drops it on the ground and grinds it out under his shoe.

"We have enough to convict him," Krauss says to Katalin. "Let's just take him outside, and I'll shoot him while he tries to escape." He says it so casually it actually scares me. I've seen Krauss in action; killing doesn't bother him.

"No," Katalin says, and my breathing resumes. "We need to make an example of this one."

Krauss picks at a piece of tobacco that's gone through his cigarette and lodged in his teeth. "You're going to hang, Calypto. One way or the other, you're done."

"So why should I help you?"

"There are easy ways to die and slow, hard ways. Open the orb."

"I told you, I don't know how to do that."

Katalin pulls the case back to her and snaps shut the lid. "Perhaps you need to think about your options." Her chair scrapes loudly as she pushes away from the table and rises. She raps on the door, and the two guards come in. "Take him back," she says and leaves with the case.

Krauss grins at me as the guards come around the table and take my arms. He blocks them from taking me away. Leaning close, he whispers, "I'll see you soon."

They return me to my cell. The bolts lock into place again, and once more I am cast into the near darkness. How did Krauss know I was going to be here, and at the auction? They were waiting for me to bid on the Celestial Orb, and are convinced that it's some sort of box containing secrets. But isn't that what it's supposed to be? Only intended for Arkady Petrescu, not me. If Krauss is looking for a traitor, it's Petrescu. Could it be this is a case of mistaken identity? Perhaps the Red Cuffs learned of the Celestial Orb from one of their spies in the Papalate, and instead of immediately seizing the item, they decided to find the traitor on this end. Unknowingly I stepped into that role when I bought it out from under Petrescu—an all too familiar case of one ministry not knowing all the facts.

A chill runs through my body. *We have enough to convict him*, Krauss said, and he might be right. Assuming he has no idea about my mission—a valid assumption—he would never believe me if I told him Arkady Petrescu, decorated war hero, head of one of the most respected families in the Empire, is the traitor he wants. Given our history, I'm not even sure if he would try to substantiate my story. Even if he did, I'm not certain The Order would admit to anything. To do so would require them to answer questions best left unasked about Petrescu and this mission, which jurisdictionally should be a Red Cuff operation. One of the first things we learn in training is that The Order will do everything in its power to prepare us for our work, but once we are in the field, we are on our own. The Order will not—cannot—compromise itself, its work, or the Empire.

Yet, no matter how convinced Krauss or Katalin are of the strength of their case, I don't see this as a clear-cut conviction, assuming of course I'm afforded any semblance of a fair tribunal. Anyone could have bought the orb thinking they were getting only an exceptional piece of art. I would like to think that, without additional evidence, a conviction would never be rendered. That's why they need me to open it, and that's precisely why I never will, for them at least. I suspect their plan is to hold me here as long as they can in the hope that they can break me.

It's El Emir all over again, except my prospects look grimmer this time because Krauss will be more vigilant than he was before.

The cell grows colder as I sit here stewing in my thoughts. The bricks must be an exterior wall, because they're colder than the others. I start pacing to warm up, but I can't escape the cold. The room is too small and the stone floor is like standing on ice. After an hour—maybe more because I can't see my watch—I decide to sit because my legs are getting sore from the hard floor. I sit on the opposite side of the cell from the brick wall, propped in the corner to the left of the door. My nose is raw and runny; my cut ear throbs, while the other is just numb. Still I wait, my arms wrapped around me, my hands tucked into my armpits to stave off the numbing cold.

My shivering interferes with any thought.

Finally, a shadow crosses the crack under the door and stops.

I don't know if I should be excited or afraid. I expect they're not bringing me a blanket and a hot meal.

A narrow panel on the door slides aside, and one of the guards peers in. He tells me to stand facing the brick wall with my arms extended outward. After I do as I'm told, the bolts slide back. The door creaks open, and several people enter.

"Turn around," Krauss says.

I shield my eyes from the bright light in the hallway. Krauss and the two guards are fuzzy shadows between me and the open door. I'm tempted to go for it, but I don't like the three-to-one odds.

Krauss makes a sharp motion with his left hand and the two guards come at me. I don't resist them. Why give Krauss any excuse to take out his anger on me? I can only hope he has orders not to damage me too severely. Krauss has no respect for life, but I believe he has respect for his chain of command.

The guards grab my arms. They are firm in their actions, but when I don't resist, they do not get rough with me. They snap cuffs around my wrists, crude metal rings with poorly filed edges that dig into my flesh. Attached to the rings are leather straps that they feed through the eye-level bolts protruding from the brick wall. They pull the straps tight enough that my arms are extended straight out from my sides and my hands are just above the level of my shoulders. They tie off the straps.

In this position, I'm forced to hold my arms up or their weight will press down painfully on the sharp edges of the wrist cuffs.

So it begins.

The guards step away. I can't tell what they think of all this from their expressions. They probably think I'm just another traitor, and thus would have few concerns about coaxing whatever information they can from me. Torture isn't an official policy of the Empire, but as they say, we're all adults here. The Red Cuffs would never openly admit to their ways, but people don't fear them because they give them hot tea and biscuits and say please when they ask questions.

Krauss steps up to me, and I consider kicking him in the groin, but his hands are ready for such an attack. Mostly, I don't want to give him the satisfaction of thwarting me.

"You're just going to take this, Calypto? Did you leave your spine in El Emir?"

I don't say anything. What is there to say after all? This is going to get unpleasant before it gets any better, if it does get better.

"You have anything you want to tell me?" Krauss asks.

I avert my eyes, but Krauss moves back into my field of view. I hate the shape of his face, the long slender nose with the little hook at the end, like a talon. His flat, square chin covered in coarse, coal-black stubble. I find his face the stuff of bad dreams.

"What's in the orb?"

His breath is bitter with the odor of tobacco.

"Who sent it to you?"

He reaches up and caresses my wounded ear like a lover might. I close my eyes, waiting for him to do something violent, but he doesn't. "I'll take your ear later," he whispers. "Unless you answer my questions."

Eventually, when I don't respond, he leaves. The guards follow him out of the cell, and Krauss watches me as they close the door and slam the bolts back into place. His face is the last thing I see before being cast back into the darkness, and every time I blink, I see his dark eyes and the pain they promise.

Already I'm cold, and my fingertips grow numb. My suit coat hangs open and the air is freezing the sweat on my torso.

It's only been a few minutes, but the muscles in my shoulders are starting to tire. Experimentally I lower my arms slowly so my wrists rest on the cuffs. The edges are sharp, but not sharp enough to cut the skin. When I let more weight down, however, the pain becomes uncomfortable. I raise my arms again.

Over the next several minutes, the ache increases in my shoulders. My arms tremble under the strain. I close my eyes and try to withdraw into myself. I seek a quiet place where I can turn off the physical pain, but I can't find it. I've never had such a place. My youth was filled with sadistic boys; my adulthood with people like Krauss. I've never had a safe place. I draw deep, regular breaths and focus on holding my arms steady, but the pain has become intense, and struggle as I might, my arms are slowly lowering. The cuffs dig into my wrists, not too painfully at first, but as they cut off the circulation to my hands, my fingers begin to throb, as if they've been struck a blow with a hammer.

I bite down hard, grinding my teeth.

Time slowly slides past. The pain increases as I can no longer hold my arms up, and their full weight rests on the cuffs. Gradually, the sharp cuffs slice through the delicate skin on my wrists, nothing deep or dangerous. The cuts burn at first, at least until that pain mingles together with all the other pain. Pinpricks of light dazzle my vision; time and place cease to exist. There is only the constant pulse of pain, pounding through my being, forcing ragged breaths in and out of my lungs as if I'm a huge bellow.

Then it ends suddenly as I drop to the floor. I hadn't realized my legs had buckled and that I was hanging from my wrists, but I must have been, because when the straps are finally, unexpectedly released, I crumple to the floor, unable to move my arms, even to break my fall. My forehead cracks on the stone tiles, but it is only another point of pain in all the other pain. The wrists cuffs are left in place, but the leather straps are removed. The bolts slide again with a loud bang, and once more I'm alone, blind and unable to move.

My body wracks with shivers.

I taste blood.

Released, my hands burn with pins and needles, and although I try to bite off any sound, I groan as I clutch them to my chest.

I think I've peed myself, but I'm not certain of anything right now, except that my misery, for the moment, has been granted a stay.

I curl into a ball. For a long time the pain is worse than when I was shackled, but as with all things, even that slowly fades to a dull ache. Eventually my arms work well enough that I'm able to wipe the snot from my nose.

My mind slowly begins to clear. I take inventory.

I have a knot on my forehead from where I hit it on the floor, but I don't think I did serious damage. My wrists are raw and sticky. My legs are cramped, likely from standing too long and from dehydration. Other than the half of a glass of vinars at the auction and the cup of water in the interrogation room, I've had nothing to drink in Coruşu. It seems as if I've been in the cold and dark a long time, but in these situations, time becomes distorted. It's just as likely I've been here three hours as three days.

I force my thoughts away from time. Thinking about its passage—the past, the future—only heightens the suffering.

Besides, I should rest while I can.

Eyes closed, I lie shivering on the floor, the darkness heavy on me like dirt in a grave. The only way I know my eyes are really closed is when the door opens, the room remains black. Boots click on the floor. If I pretend to be dead, maybe they will leave me be. Something metallic scraps across the floor, coming to a stop near my head. Then the boots retreat and the door closes again.

I count to ten before I open my eyes.

In the faint light is a tray with a cup and pieces of something that I can't quite make out in the dimness. The metal cup is filled with ice water. I force myself to drink it slowly, holding and warming each sip in my mouth before swallowing it. Even so it brings on more shivers. The dark shapes on the tray are a chunk of heavy bread, a single slice of hard cheese, and some meager bits of boiled meat—pork I think. Everything is tough, but it feels good in my stomach.

As if someone has been watching me, the door opens again as soon as I swallow my last bite. I squint into the bright light and the shadow filling the doorframe; my body quakes uncontrollably.

"This isn't how we treat people," Katalin says. There's a sharpness in her voice, almost convincing, I must admit. "Let him clean up, and then bring him to me."

The guards pull me up, but my feet are so numb I can't stand on my own. They loop my arms around their shoulders, and together we walk out into the hallway. The light is blindingly bright, making my eyes water. They take me through the door across the hall from my cell.

In a cramped alcove of the small washroom is a shower stall with no curtain. They deposit me on the alcove floor and turn the water on me. The ice-cold water burns on my skin. I scream and thrash on the shower floor, but after a few seconds the water warms, and I lie still, letting the heat soak into my limbs.

When I have enough feeling in my legs I slowly undress. Blood forms cuffs on my dress shirt, and I find blood on my collar where my ear must have started bleeding again. As I remove each article of clothing, one of the guards takes it from me.

They drop a cake of white soap at my feet, and I use it to wash my hair and the blood caked onto my wrists. A series of lateral cuts has shredded the skin and they start to bleed again as I scrub, creating a red swirl that spirals down the drain. I stay in the shower as long as I can and drink as much as my stomach will hold. Eventually I am warmed enough that I realize just how cold the shower actually is.

The guard turns off the water. "You're clean enough," he says, handing me a thin towel. "Get dressed."

My clothes have been replaced with simple trousers and a long-sleeved linen shirt. The fabric is thick and warm, but not as warm as the suit I was wearing. My shoulders ache as I shrug the soft shirt into place. There are no shoes, only a pair of soft house slippers.

Once I'm finished, I'm taken to the interrogation room, where Katalin awaits me.

"Sit down," she says, waving me toward the chair with her hand. She has beautiful hands—slender but not bony, the tips of her fingers rounded, not flattened off like my own. Her nails are trimmed to a no-nonsense length yet their strength is unmistakable.

"Where's your partner?" I ask. I stand behind the chair, not sure if I want to give her the satisfaction of sitting obediently at her command.

"I am a patient person," she says, "but these are not patient times. I can't stop them from hurting you unless you help me." A wan smile finds her lips. "But I've got a feeling you're not going to do that, are you?"

"You get a lot of feelings, don't you? Or do you just have good information on me?"

"Please, sit. We're all friends here."

We're not friends here, and I don't want to sit, but then, what's the harm in it, I think, like a little voice has whispered it in my ear. I sit, cupping my hands on the tabletop like it's my school desk.

Katalin perches on the edge of the table, turned so

one of her thighs is perched on the top and her skirt has slid up above her knee. "Lives are at stake here; I need to know what's in the orb."

"I don't know what's in the orb."

"You know what, I believe you."

"That's good because it's the truth."

"Krauss sees traitors everywhere, but I see a man who's made a mistake and would like to fix that mistake. You can fix it by telling me why you did it."

If I could have helped her, I might have made that mistake. Something in her voice is compelling, and seems to jumble my thoughts, almost as if she held some magical sway over my will. The effect is subtle, and if my defenses weren't so heightened, I might not have noticed it at all. But even if I wanted to help her, I can't because I'm not the traitor she thinks I am.

"I don't know what's in the orb or how to open it."

Katalin sighs heavily and looks downcast. She sinks into the chair across from me and rests her head in her hands.

The silence presses against my ears uncomfortably. She is waiting for me to break it, but I won't. Quiet doesn't bother me. It stretches until finally Katalin speaks.

"I don't care if you open the orb, but tell me, Calypto, why did you do it?"

I want to ask "Do what?" but don't want to engage her.

"Why do you help them? Tell me that, at least. That will be enough for me to get Krauss off you."

And enough to get me hanged. A good chance I wouldn't even get a tribunal if I admit to being a traitor.

"I'm a loyal servant of the Emperor," I say.

"Are you sure you don't want to clear your conscience?"

There is something oddly compelling about the timbre of her voice. It promises peace if only I give her what she wants. The Red Cuffs have trained her well.

"I have nothing to clear," I say.

She looks disappointed. "I've been called back to Aurestapol. I leave in an hour, and I won't be back for several days if ever." She shrugs. "Vagaries of the job; you understand. I won't be here to stop Krauss, but I can help you now. You can trust me."

I lean back in my chair, rubbing at the raw skin on my wrists. I resist the urge to call her a liar. She has no interest in helping me. I am certain of that.

After a moment, she pushes away from the table. Disappointment hangs on her like a shawl. I feel as if I should say something to remove that disappointment, but I catch my words before they cross my lips.

Katalin hesitates at the door. "It is out of my hands now." She raps smartly, and the guards let her out, closing me inside.

The woman is like no other Red Cuff I have encountered. They are usually boorish and lack subtlety, and it continually surprises me that they are effective. Maybe they aren't, based on the unrest in the central provinces. But they still have the ear of the Emperor, or so I am led to believe, and that makes them dangerous.

But Katalin is nothing like Krauss. It's as if she was chosen specifically for me. She seems to know exactly how to manipulate me, even if I'm able to resist it, but how long until I slip up?

My thoughts are jarred back to the room as the door opens again, and Krauss comes in followed by the two guards. "Now it's just you and me," he says with a grin that is a malicious slit in his face, "and no one to save you this time."

今

TIME PASSES. How much, I don't know. They shift me through a series of stress postures—hanging from my wrists again, standing up on the balls of my feet, bent over with my hands tied around the back of my knees so I can't straighten. Each is uncomfortable at first, painful after a few minutes, excruciating after a dozen. Several times I black out to be awakened with cold water. Always the cold and dark too, which is worse now that I no longer have the wool suit coat. Double so when I'm wet after they dump water on me.

This continues for what starts to feel like eternity, but I suspect it's been only a few days. I see Krauss only when he arrives to oversee a new torture. It is hard not to be impressed with his efficiency. He doesn't appear to take pleasure in what he does; more he seems to view it as a necessity to an end. Calmly he directs the guards in how to position me—"No. The shackle must be tighter ... push his head lower ... no, not so much force or you'll dislocate it ..."—and when they fail to get it exactly as he wants, he shows them. This cold efficiency is much different than the last time I was at his mercy in El Emir. He has learned something from that, no doubt.

My life becomes a series of episodes. Pain broken by too brief respites of quiet where I lie on the stone floor, unable to move, shivering and terrified that at any moment the door will open and the pain will start again. Sometimes food and water show up during these quiet moments. Other times I am simply left to my thoughts, which become more frayed, more incoherent with each passing episode. One time, I am dragged from the room and put into the shower again. This time there is no hot water, but they hold me under it and force me to wash the blood from my wrists and ankles, from my ear which Krauss has taken to pulling harshly every time before he leaves me to my private misery. After I'm clean, they put me in the interrogation room with Krauss, who sets the orb on the table in front of me.

"Open it."

The sound of Krauss's voice makes me flinch, and I feel the satisfaction radiating from him.

When I try to speak, my voice croaks hoarsely. I stop and clear my throat. It is sore, and I feel feverish. "I can't."

"Can't or won't?"

A bolt of fear goes through me. If I cannot help him, the pain will resume. I catch myself in this line of thought. He is breaking me. He's not there, yet, but how much longer will it be?

How long has it been already?

I take a deep breath, which to Krauss probably looks like resignation, but it's a way to muster my fortitude. I still have control over that. "I *can't* open it," I say more forcefully.

"I don't believe you."

"It's the—"

But he doesn't let me finish. He rises and raps on the door. When the guards open it, he says, "Hang him up." He speaks to them with such calm, without regard for me.

The words eviscerate me. This cycle will go on *ad infinitum* until I die or someone calls him off. And who will call him off? Does The Order even know what's happened to me or have they simply abandoned me? Katalin? I think she would call him off—and she seems to be in position to do it—but to do that she would want something from me, and that something could lead to a rope around my neck. At least that would be a quick end, if done right.

I squeeze shut my eyes. I can't start thinking like this. This process is about mentally breaking me to do their will; they don't want it to kill me. If they had wanted me dead, they could have done that already. They want me to open the orb and give them whatever may be inside. Yet something about that doesn't seem entirely accurate either because Katalin was willing to settle for a confession to being a traitor. That doesn't get them the contents of the orb. The only thing that ensures is me sent to the gallows.

Is this even about the orb?

"Why not just smash it?" I hear the rising panic in my voice, and even though Krauss's back is to me, I imagine his smile. "Smash it open!" I reach for the orb, but the guards seize my arms. I'm yanked from the chair and dragged down the hall. I struggle against them, but I don't have the strength to even slow them. "If you want it opened, break it! Break it!"

Krauss stands framed in the open doorway of the interrogation room. "What do you think I'm doing?" he says, grinning.

The guards shackle my hands behind my back and loop a leather strap through the eye bolt in the ceiling. With a forceful yank, they pull my arms upward, until the only way to make the pain bearable is to bend over and stand up on the balls of my feet. They secure me in this position and leave.

I try to block out the rising pain in my shoulders and legs by focusing on this new information. This isn't about the orb; this is about me. Krauss isn't the one in charge; Katalin is, and I don't think she cares what's in the orb. As I think back, I can't remember her ever asking me to open it, likely because she knows, or at least suspects, that I have no idea what it is or what's inside it. She wants me to confess, which is the easiest way to avoid a tribunal and be done with me. No fanfare, no show, no sympathy, no questions asked, and no risk of me walking away.

So why not just shoot me and bury my body where no one will find it? No one would notice. But I have no answer, and my gut tells me *this* is the real question.

The pain in my shoulders bangs at the edges of my thought, demanding attention. With each passing second, it's getting harder to ignore.

"Who would notice?" I ask myself between ragged breaths.

My legs burn now, too, and it's getting hard to stay up on my toes, but if I drop onto the flat of my feet, the pain in my shoulders increases exponentially.

"Who would notice?" I ask myself again, trying to keep my thoughts away from the pain.

Shackles of Doubt

My legs tremble under the strain.

No one that matters would notice. Unless—

My legs give out, and it feels like my arms are being ripped from their sockets.

I scream.

今

WHEN THE PAIN finally subsides, I'm lying on the floor curled into a ball. I don't remember the guards lowering me or removing the shackles. My shoulders ache, but nothing has been dislocated or broken. My calves still burn, and I doubt I can stand, so I lie shivering on the ice-cold floor, staring at the crack under the door and dreading the moment when it opens again.

As I regain control over my faculties, my breathing slows, and I become aware of a faint echo. I hold my breath, but the sound of breathing continues.

With considerable effort, I raise my head. That simple act shoots pain through my neck and shoulders.

A shadow leans against the brick wall, and it takes me a moment to recognize its shape as human because it's bent at an odd angle. The new prisoner's hands have been shackled to the wall at about the height of his face. His back is to me, allowing him to hunch over and rest his forehead against the bricks between his elbows. From where I am on the floor, he looks like a headless lump.

The shadow shifts. "So you're alive." His voice is barely above a whisper and trembles as he shivers. The accent is unmistakable, however; my cellmate is from the Papalate.

"Who are you?"

"Some courtesy you show," he says. "To not even introduce yourself. I would offer my hand, but I am currently indisposed." The shackles clink as he tries to raise his hands to prove his point.

I push myself up into a sitting position and brace myself there with my arm. Otherwise I'm not sure I could remain upright.

"My name is Carlo," he says, "but if yours is such a secret, can you at least tell me where I am?"

This is too convenient. Everything that happens to me here is well-thought out and carefully scripted, so Carlo's arrival can be no coincidence. Most likely this is another attempt to get me to confess—Carlo is probably not even a real prisoner, but a Red Cuff agent put here to bond with me and extract a jail-cell confession.

I don't know how to handle this unexpected development—and my current mental disarray does me no favors—so I decide to buy time by answering. "Coruşu," I say.

"By your accent, you're ..."

"Not Papalate."

Carlo grunts quietly. *If you are not Papalate, and you are being held in an Empire prison, then you must be a traitor.* That is what his grunt is meant to tell me in the dark.

"What happened to you?" I ask. The more he talks, the less I have to.

"Our convoy got trapped in the snow near

Yushkivech …"

I don't know the area he's describing, but I let him talk uninterrupted. He tells me a story that involves a tactical blunder on the part of his commanding officer and some bad luck with the weather and terrain, and nothing to do with the skill of the Emperor's forces. I am surprised how easily he talks and how much he says, but then, if his job is to win my trust, it's exactly what he should do.

"That was … let's see … a Tuesday … no, a Monday, but I don't know what day it is today. They kept me blindfolded, and I've been moved several times."

The auction was Sunday night. If Carlo is telling me the truth—and I have no reason to believe he is—I've been here several days, not a lifetime.

"This isn't a prison camp, is it?" His voice is tinged with fear. "I'm only a *soldato*. I do what I'm told, and they don't tell me anything I don't need to know, which is a lot. Why am I here?"

He's trying hard to appeal to my sympathies, to form a kinship bond, to convince me that we are comrades in this shared injustice and mutual misery, but I find it hard to be sympathetic when I know he is only trying to manipulate me. I must not engage him.

"Shut up," I say.

"What?"

I crawl into the corner on the opposite side of the cell and pull my legs up to my chest, hoping to trap some of my core heat. I don't want to be anywhere near Carlo. I don't want to talk to him or have him talk to me. Even if he isn't one of Krauss's spies, I would think the same way. My only hope is to hold out and stay strong, and any distraction will weaken my resolve.

"I said shut up."

"I'm only—"

"Stop talking!" I don't know where I find the strength to yell, but I don't like my reaction. Krauss is likely standing outside the door listening to our conversation. My outburst will tell him he's getting to me.

Carlo is quiet now, except for an occasional sniffle. We sit there in the dark silence; our breathing falls in to a paired rhythm. I count our breaths and guess an hour goes by.

The bolts crack on the door and scrape aside.

Instinctively, I cower into the corner, hoping they are here for Carlo and not me. Every time the door opens, I cringe away from the sound. Whenever I see Krauss, my stomach gets hollow, as if I've not eaten for a week.

The guards see me in the corner, but otherwise ignore me as one of them crosses the cell. I try to cover the sound of my relief; I don't want to attract the attention of the one who has stayed by the door. They haven't gone out their way to be rough with me, but why tempt them with any opportunity?

"Krauss wants you," the guard says to Carlo. He releases the manacles and shoves Carlo towards the door. Carlo stumbles and falls to the floor.

"Get up." The guard seizes a handful of Carlo's hair and drags him across the cell. Before he can get to the door, the hair rips free and Carlo tumbles to the floor again with a scream.

"I'll come! I'll come!" he says, protecting his head with his arms.

The guards pull Carlo to his feet and drag him out

of the cell, closing and bolting the door behind them.

I sit in the dark, straining to hear anything above my ragged breathing. They have taken Carlo to the interrogation room, I can tell that much, but once they are inside, I cannot hear anything. Part of the ruse, I bet. Treat Carlo—or whatever his real name is—poorly to further manipulate my sympathies. Krauss and Carlo are probably shaking hands now, having a good laugh, and probably sharing some vodka.

I try to relax in this moment of quiet, but it is hard with my constant shivering and the soreness of my entire body. Even so, I am in some peace because I know Krauss is otherwise occupied, and I have at least a few moments free from the constant threat of torment. This momentary peace will end, however, and too soon at that.

I don't want to think about that now. I need this respite to refortify my mind as much as time allows. When Carlo returns, I expect everything will begin anew, and with increased intensity. Krauss is getting impatient, but I cannot let him break me.

Curled up as I am, I am as comfortable as I can be in the frigid room. I allow my eyes to close, but sleep will not come. Instead my thoughts wander over the paths of my life, and I think about people who have been kind to me. The fact there are so few of them makes me sad. Their faces materialize in the darkness around me: R and, in her way, Lera, and Odella, before I ruined what we had. They are all women, and none of them are what I would call friends. My life is empty of anything meaningful, but who in my profession can have a meaningful relationship when our lives are built of lies and misinformation? I tried that once, with Odella, and it only gave me heartache and a child who thinks her father is dead. It's for the best. I am incapable of anything meaningful.

Cold streaks burn down my cheeks, and I realize I'm crying. I wipe them away in disgust, but I can't muster enough anger to stop the flow, so I let them fall, hoping to get them all out before the guards return.

Eventually my tears run out, leaving me drained and cold, like a shunt has been stabbed into me, and all my energy has been sucked away. I am weaker than I had realized, and now I am afraid. How much more I can endure?

Noise comes from the hallway, and a pit opens in my stomach. The door bolts slide back, and light floods into the cell.

The two guards drag Carlo's limp body into the room. His feet scrape on the floor behind him, occasionally moving feebly as Carlo tries to get them back under him. The guards press him face first against the brick wall and are occupied with shackling him back into the rings, leaving no one at the door. The rectangle of light cast on the floor is unbroken by shadow. The hallway is empty.

I could try for it, but the thought paralyzes me.

Krauss wants me to try, so he can justifiably shoot me, and be done with it. No guard would be so careless. This must be planned. I expect Krauss is standing in the hall, his FP ready to shred my head the moment it appears. Shot during an escape attempt; even Katalin would have to accept that if the guards corroborated the story.

Yet, at the same time, my brain screams at me to try. Staying here will be a slow, painful death. At least if I am shot in the hallway, I will have died trying to do something—killed in action, not dying in passivity.

In my weakened state, however, I cannot reconcile these competing thoughts and sit frozen in the corner, watching the guards finish shackling Carlo to the wall and turn back to the door. They don't look surprised to see me huddled in the corner, and one of them grins at me because he realizes what has transpired in my head. He knows I am breaking, and that the time is growing near when he will be done with me.

They shut the door and the two bolts bang closed with the finality of a coffin lid.

I should feel some sort of emotion—anger, disappointment, loathing—but I can muster nothing.

Nothing.

Carlo's feet scrape on the floor. In the faint light I see that he's hanging from his wrists. He's trying to stand, but his feet can't find purchase. His breathing is a wet gurgle.

I watch him from where I sit. I should help him, I realize, but I can't bring myself to.

After several feeble attempts, he manages to get his feet under him and stand. He locks his knees and leans against the wall then spits something onto the floor.

"They think a little roughing up will break me?" he asks, and I wonder if he's talking to himself or addressing me. "I used to get worse from my father." He looses a string of curses in his own language, expletives aimed at either his father or Krauss or possibly both. They are inventive, as is the way in the Papalate. I have long admired their colorful idioms and passionate invectives.

"When I get out of here, I will show them a real beating," Carlo says.

I mean to say nothing, but I make a disdainful noise.

Carlo turns as best he can in his shackles. The light from under the cell door glistens off the side of his blood-soaked face. "You don't believe me?"

"Says the man chained to the wall."

"At least they need chains to hold me."

His words cut, as bad as anything that Krauss has done to me. I had a chance, and I did not take it. I'd like to believe I didn't take it because it's what Krauss wanted me to do, but the thought nags at me that I didn't take the chance because I was afraid to.

"Why don't you tell them what they want and get it over with? Coward."

The insult lights a fire in my gut. I can't manage to get to my feet because my legs are numb from sitting on the cold floor, so I swear at him in his own language, but I'm not up to a good tongue lashing and instead offer a string of pathetic insults that would sound stupid coming from a twelve-year-old trying to sound tough.

Carlo laughs, a genuine and hearty sound. I can't help laughing with him, and when I do, Carlo laughs harder, stomping his foot on the floor. He looks foolish, chained to the wall in the dark, laughing and stomping his feet like an exaggerated caricature of a second-rate stage actor. This makes me laugh even more, so that my empty stomach hurts. Tears leak from the corner of my eyes, and burn warm paths down my checks.

"My *nonna* swears better than that, but you get marks for trying."

My laughing subsides, and I sit up. The floor is too cold to lie on for long.

"Are you … How should I say … sympathetic to our cause?" asks Carlo.

"Not at all."

"Then you are in here because of a … misunderstanding?" His voice rises as he says this; he's making light.

"Of sorts."

"I'm also here because of a misunderstanding. One between our two countries. So you see, we have more than one thing in common."

"More than one?"

"Yes," he says, dropping his voice to a whisper. "The other thing we have in common is that we're both going to get out of here."

"That's bold." My butt is nearly frozen and my legs are numb. I force myself to stand and take several hesitant steps. My legs hurt as the blood trickles into them, but they are coming back to life.

"Fortune smiles on the bold at heart," Carlo says.

The bold also meet untimely ends, but I don't say that. I walk the narrow width of the cell, touch the wall, and walk back across. Three paces are all I get, but those three steps … oh, those three steps may be the only thing keeping me sane. I walk back and forth several times while Carlo prattles on. I'm not listening to him, but he doesn't seem to care.

If he wasn't working for Krauss, I'd probably like Carlo. Or at least I would like this façade he's presenting me. I have no idea what the *real* Carlo is like. Likely I'd hate him, given he's a Red Cuff.

We are left alone for a long time. How long, I don't know, but Carlo has time to tell me about his family in Cantiano. He says he has a wife and a daughter, and that he left them behind on the small vineyard that has been in his family for twenty generations. I don't believe it, but it's a nice story. He tries to draw out my story, but even if I had been inclined to tell him anything, there's nothing for me to say. I have no family that I know of, and I'd rather not remember the orphanage where I spent an unpleasant youth.

Eventually I grow tired of walking, and sit down again. The walking warmed me, but it also tired me out. I haven't slept except in short, painful snatches since arriving here, and while they feed me, the food is always meager and sporadically scheduled to confuse my sense of time. Carlo continues to talk, but my attention can no longer focus. His voice becomes a gentle drone in the darkness that allows sleep to eventually overtake me.

I AWAKE TO ROUGH HANDS on me and thrash out in surprise, hitting one of the guards in the chest. Before I realize where I am and what I've done, fists rain down on my head and shoulders. My only chance is not to fight back and to protect myself as best I can. I cover my head but a blow hits my ear and tears the old wound open again. The beating goes on for several seconds before it subsides. By then, warm blood runs down my neck from my ear, and the side of my face from a cut open above my left eye.

I'm dragged to my feet, and I stumble as I try to get my numb legs under me.

The commotion has awakened Carlo, but he pretends to be asleep even though I can see the glint of his eye as he peers out from the crook of his elbow where his head rests. He has been standing the entire time, his hands shackled at shoulder level to the cold brick wall. How he does it, I don't know.

Krauss waits for me in the interrogation room. Our conversation is short and follows a familiar script. I take my time answering because the room is warm, and I don't want to go back to the cold, dark cell. Not yet … my fingertips are just starting to tingle. Krauss produces a flask and makes a point of opening it slowly in front of me. He watches the yearning in my eyes, the way my dry tongue slides almost subconsciously over my cracked lips.

As he drinks, his Adam's apple rises and falls, mocking my parched throat. Usually he has vodka in his flask, but the way he drinks it today, I'm not certain. Whatever it is, I want it to lubricate my sandpaper-rough tongue.

When he finishes drinking, he looks at the flask then at me, as if he's considering whether to offer it. "You don't want to talk to me? A pity, because that's what friends do. Talk. Share a drink."

The flask moves around as he speaks, and my eyes follow it.

I realize what I'm doing and force my gaze down to my hands resting atop the table. They are dirty and crusted with splotches of my own blood on my wrists, the nails split and chipped. The cuffs of the linen shirt are tattered from the sharp metal rings from which they hang me and the skin is scabby and discolored. They aren't my hands; they are someone else's. Someone I don't want to be.

"So be it," Krauss says. The top of the flask rattles as he screws it back into place. His fist raps on the door.

"Hang him up."

今

FOR LONG HOURS—it always seems like interminably long hours—I am twisted and pulled into positions in which no body should ever be. Never the same one twice, and each one seemingly worse than the last. Between these eternities of suffering are moments in which the pain is allowed to slowly leak from my body along with my resolution. The bolts slide, the sound a knife in my resolve, and they string me up again like a calf being bled. I would think Carlo's presence would be a comfort. What better way to get my friendship than comfort me during those interstitial spaces between the torture, but Carlo is no comfort because when I am released from my torment, he takes my place. By the time I am aware enough to see through the searing afterimages of pain, he is already deep into his own well of suffering.

Carlo's screams are as painful on my psyche as the chains and cuff are on my body. I'd like to think I handle the torment better, but, I do not.

In the time since he's come here, I've become less certain he works for the Red Cuffs. The guards are more brutal with him than they are to me. Krauss seems to take particular pleasure in beating him because he always returns from the interrogation room bloodied and unable to walk. Maybe it's part of the show, but the injuries seem deep and real.

今

The cycle rolls on. I am not able to track the number of times I am strung up and cut down. In the dark, time distorts. All that exists is pain and less pain. Every so often the cycle breaks when I'm dragged to the interrogation room. There I quietly listen to Krauss's latest attempt to get me to confess. These meetings should be something to look forward to because the room is warm and there isn't any physical pain administered to my deteriorating body. Yet these sessions are excruciating because Krauss is there, prancing about with a smug smile, and my hate for him has started to eat at my soul. He is the reason I suffer, and the only way I see this ever stopping is for me to kill him, but I know I will never get the chance.

"Just let me die," I want to say so many times.

But he shakes his head as if truly, genuinely disappointed, and raps sharply on the door.

"String him up."

AND THE CYCLE CONTINUES. But for how much longer?

今

I HUDDLE IN THE CORNER when the guards return
Carlo to the cell and shackle him to the wall next to
me. He hangs from his wrist, groaning, his face a
collage of blood and bruises. I would think him dead
if not for his wet, gurgling breaths. After several
minutes, he struggles to his feet and props himself
against the bricks.

In his time here, he's never been free of those
shackles. Unable to sit or lie down, he sleeps hanging
by his wrists or leaning against the wall. I don't know
how he does it, and I've developed an admiration for
his strength and dedication, doubly so if he is truly a
Red Cuff.

"My *nonna* hits harder than Krauss," Carlo says,
when he catches me looking at him.

"You're *nonna* must be quite a woman."

"She could kick the Devil to Hell and back." His
grin transforms into a grimace, and we share a
restrained laugh because Carlo cannot do much more.

"I need you to do something for me," he says then,
his voice lowering. He steps on the heel of his right

shoe with his left, and lifts his foot out of it. Like me, they have replaced his original shoes—a soldier's boots in his case—with a lightweight slipper that provides no warmth and makes an ineffective sap.

"Inside," he says.

Curious I pick up the slipper. Something rolls around inside. Fishing it out, I find a small sliver of metal—a carpenter's finishing nail, the small head still black with blood.

"It took a long time, but I finally worked it free from under the table. Give it here." He clicks his index finger and thumb together. "I'm getting out of here. Are you with me?"

He takes the nail from me and twists the cuffs around so he can drive the metal sliver into the slot between the locking mechanism and the teeth.

"You're getting out of here?"

He tightens the cuff and drives the nail in further until it catches again. With a twist of his arms, the cuff opens. He grins at me. "I was … how do you say it … a delinquent in my youth."

I step away from Carlo. Is this another Red Cuff ploy? Nothing else has worked, so has Krauss come up with this plan to catch me in the act of escaping, or is Carlo who he says he is, and this is a legitimate chance at freedom? I am torn with indecision.

Carlo frees his other wrist. "I'm going to pretend I'm still cuffed. When the guards come in, I'll take the one nearest me; you take the other."

"I—"

"Surprise is on our side. You've done this before, no?"

"Escaped from a secret torture facility with an enemy soldier?"

"I don't know how you do it … keep your sense of funny."

I would have arched an eyebrow, if my face didn't ache so much.

"You've been trained to fight, yes?" asks Carlo. "Aren't all of you trained as babies to kill?"

I can't tell if he's being funny. Given the nature of the world in which we live, every child in the Empire learns to defend himself, whether through formal instruction or an education of necessity. As a member of The Order, I've been trained in numerous forms of combat, including hand-to-hand fighting. Combat has never been my strength, but I have learned enough that I can generally hold my own.

"What about Krauss?"

"I overheard him say he had to meet the train. He is gone for now, so I think it is just the two guards. Now is the best chance."

I don't know if that's true. I've never seen anyone but the same two Red Cuffs, and I've always suspected this place was built specifically for me. That doesn't make me special. Temporary, easy-build-easy-dismantle interrogation centers make tracking Red Cuff activities that much harder.

"How long ago?"

Carlo shrugs. The effort plainly causes him significant discomfort.

I wonder how far we are from the train station. It seems unlikely this facility would be in the heart of Coruşu, but I don't think the city is large. I don't remember it taking a long time to get here from the Guild Hall, although I admit my memory of that night is now fuzzy and distorted.

"Are you with me?" Carlo asks. "I need to know."

"I don't know."

"You'll die here. With Krauss gone, this is our best chance."

"Okay," I say, but I can hear the indecision in my own voice. I suspect Carlo can too, because he studies my face in the near darkness. I look away from him so he can't see my eyes. Carlo is right. I'm the only one who is going to rescue me at this point. If no one has come yet, no will be coming. It's better to get shot escaping than to die slowly in this black hole.

"I'm in," I say with more conviction.

"Good. I knew I could count on you. Here goes."

I want to ask what he's planning, but I don't get the chance. Carlo lets out a scream that nearly deafens me. "My arm!" and he follows that with a string of curses in his own language.

His screaming is so convincing I forget for a moment this is an act and come to his side. He motions me away with his eyes, and I step back. Carlo screams again and writhes in his loosened shackles as if he is almost overcome with pain.

The slot on the door slides back, revealing eyes.

"It's broken—goddammit it's broken!" Carlo screams.

The bolts slide and the door opens. I scuttle away from Carlo, my shoulders hunched and head down, trying to look as meek as possible.

Carlo screams again.

The first guard in ignores me, his attention fixed on Carlo. The second guard stays near the door. He gives me only a cursory glance, and his attention returns to Carlo when I crouch and cover my head with my arms as if trying to shield out the light coming through the door and muffle Carlo's screaming. My muscles tighten to the point of being painful.

Through the crook of my elbow, I see Carlo reposition his feet on the floor, but the move is subtle. The casual observer would have missed it with the rest of the show Carlo is putting on. When the guard is directly behind him, Carlo turns suddenly, driving his fist upward with all his strength into the guard's chin, knocking him to the ground. I leap at the second guard and slam into his lower back. Using all my weight I drive through him. We crash into the wall, and the guard's body absorbs the force of the blow, but even so, we both tumble together to the ground, and I'm slightly dazed. I don't know if I've knocked him out, but the guard isn't moving. He may just be stunned, but before I can do anything else, Carlo grabs my arm and drags me toward the door. I scramble across the floor, following him into the hallway. Carlo skids to a stop and slams shut the door that bounces in its frame as a guard bumps against it, but Carlo's weight is enough to keep it from opening. He slaps at the bolt, but it doesn't catch as the guard shoulders the door again.

I jump to my feet and shove my shoulder to metal.

Carlo locks one bolt in place then the second.

Hands on my knees, I suck air greedily. Sweat pours off me, but not because it's warm in the hallway. My eyes hurt from the bright light.

"Good job in there," Carlo says between heavy breaths.

The guard bangs away on the cell door. His threats sound comical through the metal.

"Let's go," I say, but when I straighten, my head spins, forcing my hands back onto my knees.

"Are you okay?"

"Just a little winded, but I'm good now," I say, straightening a second time.

Carlo nods. "This isn't exactly a health spa."

We turn away from the interrogation room then carefully peer around the heavy curtain that blocks the hallway. On the other side, several doors line an otherwise dark corridor. Unlike the steel door on our cell, they are stout wooden ones with decorative panels and intricate brass handles and locks. When Carlo stops at the first one, I grab his arm.

"Not that way," I say, and nod further down the hallway. When they brought me here, we came up one flight of stairs and twenty-two steps down this hallway to the prison cell.

As we move away from the curtain, the hallway grows darker. The lights have been smashed and the only illumination seeps meagerly around the black curtain behind us. It must be night outside because I would expect some light coming from under the doors lining the corridor, but the rooms beyond are dark. I count twenty-two steps and on the left is an alcove with a wide flight of stairs spiraling downward. On the right, the stairs continue upward.

We hustle down as quickly as our unsteady legs allow. The stairs prove more challenging than I expected, and if not for the adrenaline shooting through my veins, I would have tumbled headlong down them. Carlo is moving better, but not by much.

Given our condition, I'm amazed we overpowered the guards.

The stairs open into a wide, dark lobby filled with stone columns and marble floors. A long counter of thick wood runs the length of the wall opposite the stairs; some of the wood has been ripped away, leaving jagged holes in the counter's front. A tear-shaped hearth stands cold and black in the center of a ring of couches and stuffed chairs badly faded by the elements. The room is frigid; the front doors hang askew on damaged hinges. The glass is broken in a series of large, arching windows that used to let morning sunlight stream into the lobby of this once-opulent hotel.

Our feet crunch through the debris. As we cross to the doors, the air gets colder; our breath swirls around our heads like vaporous spirits.

I wrap my arms around me, but the wind coming in through the broken windows cuts into me. Our cell was cold, but outside the wind will be a worse enemy.

I grab Carlo's arm. "We need to wrap up in something."

"There's nothing, and we have no time to search."

How long can we last outside in the elements? Yet the longer we stay here, the worse our chances of escape. It is a desperate gamble with neither outcome promising, but I'd rather face the cold night than Krauss's wrath.

Outside it's colder than I expected. The night is clear. Overhead the stars are bright and crisp. The snow clings in an unblemished blanket to everything but the walkway and the road. As with all snow that's been down for a while in a city, it's lost its luster, but it still reflects the starlight and gives the night a twilit quality.

The adjacent buildings are shadowy boxes of brick and stone, many boarded up or with broken windows. They have been partially cannibalized for their metal or brick, and I would suspect nothing of value has been left inside. The snow in the street has not been cleared, but a few lines of auto tracks mar it. A narrow path of trampled snow leads from our door to the road. Across the street is a swath of trees, most naked of their leaves, but with a few conical evergreens, white in their winter coats.

We must be near the river, perhaps in an outlying area of Coruşu that has fallen on hard times thanks to the war. This close to the front, the city is dark, so I can't see any signs of Coruşu's center. But if this is the Oka River then it runs through the heart of it, and all we need do is follow it.

Carlo points across to the trees. "We'll need to confuse our tracks," he explains.

I tuck my hands into my armpits for warmth. We won't have much time before the cold takes us, but Carlo is right. We can't simply walk away without leaving a trail a child could follow.

Before we start down the steps, however, an auto rolls up out of the dark. Its headlamps are out or we would have noticed it sooner; we might have heard it, if the wind had not been blowing, but neither of us saw it until it rolled to a stop in front of us.

I push Carlo back inside, but too late. A voice cries out from the street for us to stop. The sound cuts through the wind like only Krauss's voice can.

Carlo stands mindlessly just inside the doorway, frantically searching the lobby for a place to hide. Genuine fear etches his face, and for the first time I am certain he is not a Red Cuff.

"Upstairs," I hiss. "We'll go out a window."

My words snap him out of his momentary paralysis, and he jumps forward.

Three more people have gotten out of the auto.

Krauss is already running through the snow toward the entry, his FP drawn.

In our panic, the pain and fatigue that wrack my limbs are forgotten. I take the stairs two at a time, but even in my haste, Carlo quickly passes and pulls ahead of me. I reach the first landing and nearly run into him as he stands in the middle of the corridor. "All boarded up," he says, pointing to the window at the end of the hallway. He continues to the next floor.

I open my mouth to call for him, but cut off my words. Behind me, feet scrabble through the lobby below. Krauss issues curt orders to find us.

I continue upward, although I have no idea where this will get us. From the first floor, we could have safely jumped out a window. From the second? We'll need find a fire escape or maybe the snow is deep enough ...

I reach the next landing, and Carlo is there. His eyes are wide and wild as he paces across the small alcove. This floor appears to have the same layout as the one below, except the stairs end here. We have nowhere else to go.

"Fire escape," I say. I follow the corridor to the back of the building. It ends at a window, but where I would expect to find a fire escape, there isn't one. The metal has likely been scavenged for the war effort.

I hurry back to the other end of the hallway. As I pass the stair alcove, I hear voices on the floor below.

By the time I reach Carlo, he's got the front window open and one leg out over the sill. I grab his shirt, but he brushes off my hand.

"There's a landing below," he says, ducking his head out.

I crane my head to see around him. The auto sits

down in the street, its doors standing open. Over the window on the floor below us is a steep, snowy, gable. It reaches up to within a meter of our windowsill. Below the gable is a sloping roof that covers the front porch. They all create a series of short but treacherous drops to the ground below.

Carlo's feet sink into the snow on the gable. I'm not sure what he plans to do from here, but it quickly becomes apparent, intentional or otherwise. He totters as his feet slide on the steep sides. Twisting his body, he manages to squat with his feet forward and slide down the gable, dropping off the end in a shower of snow to the porch roof below. Unable to stop his descent, he then slides to the end of roof and drops to the ground at the front of the hotel. He lands awkwardly, and rolls into the snow grabbing his ankle.

He looks up at me, and motions for me to follow.

Voices echo up the steps.

I swing my leg out the window. It's a short drop to the gable, and Carlo's descent has already cleared some of the snow. I drop onto the icy shingles. My feet slide, but I hold myself steady by the windowsill. Now I just need to do what Carlo did, and hope for the best. I turn and squat, but before I get balanced, I start to slide. I fall back on the seat of my pants. Sliding off the edge of the gable, I extend my legs to cushion my landing, but my right foot hits before my left and slips away. I tumble over with a clatter and roll down and off the sloping roof, landing with a thud in snow.

For a moment I lie there, dazed.

Carlo tugs at my arm. "Come on," he whispers urgently, and he limps off toward the street, favoring the ankle he twisted on his own descent.

I sit up, shaking snow from my hair and shivering. Carlo is already halfway down the walk. As he nears the street, another man in a heavy parka climbs out of the auto, raising a pistol.

Carlo springs forward, seizing his wrist. His momentum carries them both back against the auto.

I dash forward to help, reaching the two as Carlo tries to wrestle the pistol free. The parka hood slides back and in the reflected starlight, I see I am mistaken about our attacker. Katalin strikes Carlo in the throat with her free left hand, stunning him long enough to wrest free her pistol. She raises it, but for some reason hesitates, giving me time to strike her arm just above her wrist. The force of the blow must have caught her by surprise because the weapon flies from her hand and tumbles across the hood of the auto and into the snow on the other side. Carlo swings, but Katalin steps inside his punch. She grabs at his throat, but gets only his shirt collar as Carlo twists away. The linen rips, leaving her clutching a tattered square of cloth.

I sweep my foot out and catch the back of Katalin's knee, buckling her left leg and sending her teetering backward as Carlo swings a second time. He catches her with a glancing blow on the side of her head and she tumbles awkwardly against the side of the auto before falling to the snow.

My breathing comes in heavy blasts, and I take a moment to collect myself. In that moment, a sudden wave of disorientation comes over me. The world shifts and twists as the auto and the snow and the starry night come out of alignment. Everything seems to stick for a moment in time before ratcheting forward. I don't hesitate. I roll to the ground as a high-pitched whine buzzes by my ear and several flechettes spark off the roof of the auto. I scramble back to my feet, pivoting to locate the shooter.

Krauss leans out of the top floor window.

More flechettes shriek by as I dive through the auto's open door onto the back seat. Carlo rolls over the hood and drops behind it for cover. Several flechettes tear through the leather seating where my leg was a second before. I slide across the seat and out the open door on the other side.

On the floor of the backseat is the case containing the Celestial Orb.

"Run for it!" Carlo breaks into a limping sprint across the street toward the trees. His movement draws Krauss's fire, giving me an opening. I grab the case and sprint at an angle from Carlo. My feet pound the snow, and I hug the briefcase to my chest with both arms. I don't slow when I reach the trees, crashing headlong through the naked branches and over the snow-covered bushes. My lungs burn in the cold air, but I don't slow until I'm well into the copse and hear nothing but the tumbling of the river ahead of me and the ragged explosions of my breathing. Only then do I allow myself to slow down.

I strain to hear sounds of pursuit, but I'm also listening for Carlo. I move parallel to the river back in the direction where Carlo would have entered the trees. Already my shoes are soaked though, my wet feet numbing quickly.

"Carlo?" I whisper, and continue forward when I hear no response.

Under the trees, the darkness is deep but not absolute, and the blanket of snow deadens all sound except the crunch of my feet. I should be running away from Krauss, but I was wrong about Carlo, and I owe him.

A faint groan to my right catches my attention, and I turn in that direction. "Carlo?" I call again, even quieter now. Voices carry into the woods from the street. Krauss is organizing the men for a search. I have only seconds before I'll need to flee if I'm going to have any chance, but I must try one last time.

The groan sounds again, and I move forward quickly. In the dark I nearly fall over Carlo, who is sitting with his back against a tree trunk, his legs sprawled before him like dropped twigs. I kneel next to him and set the briefcase down in the snow at his side.

Carlo clutches the base of his neck. His hand glistens as blood flows out between his fingers. Already the front of his shirt is soaked and steaming in the cold. His mouth moves in a gulping motion like a fish out of water. "Hold on, Carlo," I say, pushing my own hand against his to stem the blood pulsing out.

With his other hand, Carlo grabs my forearm. He stares at me with glassy eyes. "Petrescu," he says, and as if he thought I hadn't heard him, he repeats the name again, this time a little louder. Then he grimaces, and his grip on my forearm weakens. With his last breath, he whispers one final word, "Orb."

The blood flow grows less. My hands are sticky and warm. I stare at Carlo, uncertain if I had heard his final words correctly. How could he know about the orb or Petrescu? Could I have mumbled something in my pain-hazed state? It's possible, but why would it mean anything to Carlo? I draw away my hand, and

Carlo's body slumps forward. On the pale skin of his back, just above Carlo's shoulder blade, is a mark that seems to glow in the faint snow light. It looks like an inverted vee with a horizontal line inside of it and two more lines beneath it connected at a right angle. It's the same tattoo as on Dai Li's neck.

My breath leaves me. Carlo wasn't working for Krauss—the escape wasn't a set-up to get me killed. Carlo must have been here to get me and the orb out of prison. But then what? Was he to deliver me to Arkady Petrescu, and does that mean Petrescu is a Silver Tiger?

The guards searching for me grow closer. Their voices carry through the trees as they coordinate their search of the copse. I'm so cold I'm wracked with shivers now. I have no choice but to leave Carlo. It seems wrong to allow the Red Cuffs to have his body, but I have no other options. I take the case and flee toward the river, away from Krauss and his Red Cuffs, and Carlo and all he represents.

I don't know where I am or where I'm going, so I simply follow the noise of the river until I come to a steep embankment that drops into the gorge that holds the icy flow. Across the river are more trees and behind those, the dark shapes of snow-topped buildings. Ice rimes the riverbanks on both sides, but the water in the middle is unfrozen and moving swiftly. In the dark and with the trees, I can't see far either up or down stream.

I close my eyes for a moment and try to remember my approach to Coruşu. I came in from the southeast and crossed the river flowing to the west into the heart of the city. Mélon and I had walked along the river bank, and it wasn't until I passed the bridge that the river had dropped into the ravine. Therefore, I'm still on the north bank and west of the train station and Corușu proper. I turn east and work my way along the edge of the gorge where the trees are thinner, and I can see the river on my right.

A tree branch cuts my cheek as I stumble over the snowy, rocky terrain. I have to move quickly because I doubt I will last more than thirty minutes in the cold night. Behind me, one of my pursuers lets up a call. They've found Carlo. Soon they will find my footprints leading down to the river's edge and figure out which direction I have taken. I have only minutes, I would guess, until they close the noose around me.

Moving along the river is too slow and difficult, so I take a chance and cut back to the road. I can't be more than a few blocks from the old hotel, but it's too dark to see if the auto is still parked in front. Other than a set of parallel lines through the snow, it looks like no has been through here in many hours.

I sprint across the street into an alley between two buildings. The alley is narrow enough that the overhanging eaves of the buildings nearly touch, effectively blocking most of the falling snow from reaching the uneven stones. The wind has blown what snow has reached the ground into snaking windrows that I easily avoid. I try the first door I come to, and I'm rewarded when the handle turns.

Inside, a single large room is filled with empty shelves extending to the windows fronting the street. It's as cold as an ice locker, and the air is still and musty. Stairs in the back go up to a second-floor office with an old desk and a couch covered with a dusty throw. I pull the blanket off the couch—the kicked-up dust tickles my nose—and wrap it around my head and shoulders. My numb hand can barely hold it closed at my neck.

On the back wall is another door and stairs leading down to the service alley that runs parallel to the front street. Near the walls of the buildings, there isn't any snow, so I work my way down the alley, leaving no footprints. The street I cross has snow that has been trampled by many vehicles and feet, and I am satisfied I have left no trace of my passage. I continue down the service alley, trying doors as I go. Locked. Locked.

Finally, a handle turns. I crack the door, and I'm greeted with a warm puff of air. I want to throw myself inside, but I force myself to stay there, listening. I count slowly to ten. When I don't hear anything, I widen the crack enough to slip inside. The room smells sweet and doughy.

After a moment, my eyes adjust to the even deeper darkness of the room. A wide table stands along the near wall and toward the front of the room is a large display case. Warmth radiates from a stone hearth in the corner. I cross to it and stand close to the large iron door on the front of the oven and let the heat slowly seep into me.

My limbs tingle painfully, but I embrace it. Pain means I am alive.

For the first time in a long while, I am warm. With the cold gone, the pain that fills my body is finally able to move to the fore. My muscles cramp, every bruise is tender, every cut stings, and every nerve, abused by many days of torment, screams out. The pain doubles me over, and I collapse to the floor. The stones are warm, like an embrace, and I curl into a tight ball, and lay there trying not move because each shift of my muscles draws forth more hurt.

Krauss did this to me, and while I lie there, bathed in pain, I envision turning the tables on him, stringing him up as he did me, and then dancing to the music of his agony. If justice is true, Krauss will suffer tenfold what he's done to me—to Carlo—and so too will Katalin.

Eventually, urgency drives me to sit up. I don't know the time, but I doubt I have long before the baker arrives to start the day. With a grunt, I get to my feet. My stomach aches from its emptiness. A small lantern stands on the counter and I light it, turning the flame low so it casts only a small halo of illumination. Thick curtains cover the front windows, but I don't want to take more risks than are absolutely necessary. Searching, I find an old loaf of crusty bread and a pastry filled with some sort of sweet walnut paste. In an icebox, I find a bottle of buttermilk, but it's too rich for my stomach, so I drink water.

The sink is large enough and has a warm tap, so I wash myself. I'm appalled at how dirty I am—blood and dirt and urine all caked to me. If I hadn't lived in the filth, my own odor would have watered my eyes. I use the bar of hand soap to wash my hair. Hanging on a hook is a long-sleeved shirt, dusty with flour, and an apron. The shirt fits loosely, and I need to roll the sleeves or they fall to cover my hands. The bones in my wrist stretch my skin.

I wash my trousers as well as I can and hang them on the front of the oven to dry. It's probably foolish to have risked washing them, but I can't bear to wear them any longer in their current state.

As I wait for them to dry, my stomach now full, my aching body warm, I turn to the briefcase on the floor. Sitting on the warm hearth stones, I crack open the case. The Celestial Orb glitters in the lantern light. I've never held it before, and it's heavier than I expected, as if it's a solid piece of porcelain. It's warm from having rested near the oven since my arrival, but for some reason, I believe it would be warm even if it hadn't. It seems to have a radiance that exceeds the lamplight reflecting off it. The surface isn't smooth— the lettering and numbers on the rings are raised, feeling like bands of lace that circle the orb. I feel no line that suggests the orb has two halves or any sort of hinge. The rings turn easily, rotating the numbers and the months of the year around the orb. On one side the rings align to spell out a date—day, month, year—that can be changed into an infinite number of possibilities. If this is a puzzle box, as many seem to think, then these rings are the tumblers and the combination must be some date. But if the note that had accompanied the orb at the auction is to be believed, the combination is unknown, and no one has ever opened it.

Yet Petrescu seemed to want it, and Carlo's dying breath was a plea to take it to him. Could he know the combination?

I'm supposed to return the orb to Mélon, but I want answers, and Petrescu is the one who has them. But the mission … R always says finish the mission. It's more important than any personal agenda. A month ago I would have agreed with her, but now I'm not certain. Besides, this isn't a personal agenda anymore; Carlo was a Silver Tiger. Petrescu must be one too. That makes them more than disgruntled farmers and petty merchants. The Silver Tigers cannot be ignored any longer.

After twenty minutes, my pants are warm and dry.

I decide to keep the baker's shirt because I don't have the will to put my old, tattered and bloodstained one back over my shoulders. Once I've cleaned up the mess I made at the sink, I return the lantern to where I found it. Then I slip back into the alley and dump my old shirt into a refuse pile. The cold bites at my knuckles clutching the handle of the case, and I regret having to leave the warmth of bakery, but I need to get to Petrescu before Krauss and Katalin figure out where I'm going.

PART III

QUIETLY INTO THE NIGHT

THE PETRESCU MANOR sits atop a knoll of granite
lording over the center of Coruşu. A narrow road,
plowed and free of snow, climbs the north side,
where the rock slopes more gently to the surrounding
plain than on the other faces. About halfway up, a
steel bar blocks the road. A guard sits, semi-alert, in a
small shack to the side warming his hands over a few
meager lumps of coal in a brazier. Still wrapped in the
dusty blanket, I leave the road and creep past him
using a line of low trees and shrubs for cover. Once
around a bend and out of sight, I return to the road
and continue upward. I reach the top as the first light
of the dawn brightens the cloud pack to the east.

The manor sits pushed up against the south cliff,
giving it an impressive view of the city and river
below. The house is large and ancient, two floors built
of dark timber and granite, the stone likely mined
from the knoll itself. Withered vines of ivy spider-web
the outer walls, looking like cracks in the early
morning light. A steep roof holds a blanket of snow,
except near the smokestack at the west end. The

windows are shuttered and dark, but if that is because the occupants are asleep or blackout curtains are in place, I cannot say.

Now that I am here, standing in the drive, stamping my feet for warmth, I don't know what to do. I haven't thought much beyond getting to Petrescu. Now that I'm here, do I simply knock on the door and ask what he knows about the orb or perhaps rip the collar of his shirt away and yell, "Aha! You are a Silver Tiger!" And who else might be in the house with him? His wife, surely, but any servants or bodyguards? I saw none at the auction, but they might have given him more space at a secure function, and any number of the people along the wall could have been Petrescu's retinue.

But the hour is early, and from the smoke climbing lazily from the western chimney, someone is up, so that is as good a place as any to start.

Bent low, but moving quickly, I approach the house. A stone walk that has been shoveled goes west along the front of the manor and circles around to the back. I follow the trail, taking care to stay off the undisturbed snow. In the back, a veranda perches on the edge of the cliff. During summer, when the evenings are warm and thick, it must provide an inspiring view of the city and the distant countryside. Now the shadow from the house casts it into unwelcoming darkness, and a wind blowing up from the city below leaves me fiercely cold.

Sticking close to the wall where the shadow is darkest, I creep down to a door. To my surprise it is unlocked. I bury the blanket in the snow piled against the side of the building, and slip into a warm chamber, closing the door quickly behind me to keep out the cold. The room, apparently a prep room off the kitchen, is unlit except for a faint light that comes through an open doorway to my right. In the adjoining kitchen, a round woman in a dusty apron hums a mournful song as she kneads dough on a wooden counter top with her thick hands. Entranced by her work, she doesn't notice as I cross the open doorway and slip out into the main hallway.

The inner sanctum of the house, away from windows, is lit by wall sconces. A rich red carpet muffles the sound of my feet as I creep down a hallway toward the door at the west end. I pass several other doors, all of them closed to keep the light in and the chill out. On the walls hang portraits of solemn men and women—Petrescu's, or maybe his wife's, ancestors.

Away from the kitchen, the house is quiet, except for a faint clacking emanating from behind the western door. The noise grows louder and sharper as I approach. The door is cracked open about a hand's breadth.

Cautiously, I peer inside. Arkady Petrescu sits at an imposing desk of dark wood pounding away on the keys of a typewriter.

I take a deep breath and step inside, closing the door completely behind me. Petrescu, hearing the latch click, looks up from the keys. The typewriter jams as his fingers falter, and he looses a surprised curse.

"I mean no harm, and I only want to talk," I say in as calm a voice as I can muster. I hold up the case for him to see.

Petrescu removes his reading glasses from their perch on his nose, folds the temples, and sets them on the desk. He squints at me. "Mr. Tolnovski?" he asks, just now recognizing me. Battered and bruised, scruffy with several days of growth, wild-haired and probably equally wild-eyed; I no longer resemble the man he met at the auction. For most, I would have made a frightening intruder, but Petrescu's face is a mask of calm. I suspect he has a pistol in his desk drawer, but I also doubt he would need it if this encounter came to violence.

"May we sit?" I motion to a pair of chairs before the fire.

"I prefer to stay here," he says, confirming my suspicions about the weapon. He motions to a less comfortable looking chair near his desk.

I cross the room slowly, sit and lay the briefcase across my lap. "I appreciate your discretion," I say.

Petrescu acknowledges my gratitude with a nod. "What can I do for you, Mr. Tolnovski?"

"To start, I think we should drop the games and pretenses," I say. "My name is not Dimitri Tolnovski. I am employed by the Emperor's grace and in his service. I was sent to obtain this item as evidence against you as a spy."

Petrescu's eyebrows rise. He sits back suddenly.

His surprise seems genuine.

"I'm not a spy," he says.

I click the latches on the briefcase and open the top then remove the Celestial Orb and hold it up. "I want to know what's inside this, so I propose we open it here, together."

Petrescu steeples his fingers. He seems to have recovered from the initial shock of having his loyalty questioned by a stranger who claims to be part of the government he has spent his life serving. "I don't know what you're talking about," he says. "Before the auction, I had never seen that before. I buy pretty baubles, that is all."

He is a convincing liar, and doubt seeps into me like water. I return the orb to the case as if our discussion is over. I hope this show of me preparing to leave convinces him to negotiate, but he says nothing as I click the latches back into place.

I hesitate on the edge of the seat, but Petrescu simply watches me over his fingertips. "I don't know what the Silver Tigers hope to achieve," I say, "but I know this orb is important. Are you sure you won't reconsider?"

"Honestly, Mr. Tolnovski or whatever your real name is, I don't know what you are talking about. You come in here and question my loyalty to the Empire and talk like a crazy man. I should shoot you, and if I was the spy you say I am, I would certainly do that, but it's early, and I'm a charitable man."

I'm not entirely sure if he's joking. No one would blink if he did shoot me dead, but based on what I know about the man, he would require considerably more impetus to pull a trigger and end a life. Petrescu is an honorable man; he has been all his life. He loves the Empire, and the only reason he would do anything against it is if he truly felt it would make the country a better place.

"We are done here," Petrescu says, rising. "I will show you to the door."

With no ideas, I am resigned to leaving. My mind is a jumble of disappointment, and I am unable to think clearly, so my body simply moves of its own accord. Rise. Walk to the door.

Petrescu collects his cane from where it leans

against his desk and stumps behind me.

At the other end of the hallway we come to a foyer. A wide cascade of carpeted stairs with ornately carved balustrades tumbles down in a sweeping curve from a landing above. The foyer's ceiling vaults all the way to the roof. Across from me, a hallway, much the mirror image of the one down which I've just walked, extends into the east wing of the manor. To the left is the main door out to the front drive.

"I suggest you leave Coruşu on the next train and never return," Petrescu says.

As he reaches for the door handle, however, the bell rings.

Petrescu freezes, seemingly uncertain what to do. I consider the time and wonder who would be calling at such an hour. Surely no one making a purely social visit.

Catherine Petrescu comes sweeping down the stairs in a robe and doesn't notice either her husband or me before she reaches the bottom of the stairs. Then she draws back suddenly, her face blanching noticeably, as if confronted by a significant horror. She stifles a scream and grips the banister. "Oh, Arkady, I didn't know you had a visitor."

She doesn't seem to recognize me or the case I'm holding.

"He's leaving," Petrescu says. "Were you expecting someone? At this hour?"

Catherine smiles at her husband. I have become a non-entity in her world. "An old friend passing through," she says, as if that explains everything.

Petrescu arches an eyebrow. His shoulders rise in a quick shrug, and I get the impression this is not entirely an unusual an occurrence. He opens the door.

A woman stands on the porch, wrapped in a deep blue cloak with the hood pulled over her head. Petrescu steps aside to let her enter, and her boots click loudly on the tiles. She and Catherine embrace tentatively, not as old friends might, but in a fashion of politeness and feigned cordiality, like two rivals of high, but equal standing.

Petrescu clears his throat and motions toward the door with a curt sweep of his arm.

"Thank you for seeing me so early," the hooded woman says, her voice hushed. "There isn't much time."

Her voice stops me in my tracks.

She lowers her hood, revealing the back of her head and thick blond hair wound into a tight bun atop a tattoo that has haunted my thoughts ever since I first saw it in Olesk.

"Dai Li?" I say before I can stop myself.

That moment, as she slowly turns from Catherine to face me, stretches into what seems to be several long minutes as I watch every change in her expression moving like a film running quarter speed. Her eyebrows, barely more than penciled-in lines, arch upward as her eyes widen and her jaw drops open. Then time clicks back into its proper speed and her expression of utter surprise vanishes as if it had never existed.

"Now this is unexpected," she says.

"You know him?" It's Petrescu's turn to be surprised.

The cold continues to swirl in through the open door.

"Close the door, Arkady" Catherine says, her eyes fixed on me now for the first time. They hold me in my spot, like a rifle in the hands of sharpshooter would. Recognition glimmers into them, and her gaze drops immediately to the case in my hand.

It becomes clear to me then. I had the wrong Petrescu. Foolish of me to assume it was Arkady Petrescu whom I wanted. In all likelihood, he is exactly what he appears to be: a loyal citizen of the Empire.

"What is going on here?" Petrescu asks.

Catherine takes her husband's arm. I watch her lead him back toward his office in the west wing of the manor, talking quietly with him.

"Don't worry about him," Dai Li says. "Catherine is very persuasive. She'll handle him. She always has."

My muscles are wound tight like a spring. Ever since Dai Li left me in Olesk, I've wanted to find her and get answers to my questions about the Silver Tigers and their role in all this.

"You have the orb, I see," Dai Li says. "Two birds …" Her lips slide into a smile that scares me. "We should talk."

"You read my mind."

She leads me down the east hallway to a small sitting room decorated for a woman: delicate furniture, all fluid curls and floral cloth, matching wallpaper, painted landscapes and still lifes hung in ornate frames. Marble sculptures, jeweled boxes, and gleaming metal abstractions littering every horizontal surface. Above the fireplace, a mantel clock ticks loudly, counting off the seconds.

Dai Li closes the door behind us.

"She is quite the collector," I say, looking at a small portrait above the day bed.

Dai Li makes a disapproving sound.

Her presence pushes against my back like something tangible and solid. While my back may be to her, all my attention is on her, and the details of the picture in front of me go unseen.

"You were right," I say.

"About what?"

"About things not going so well this time." When she doesn't respond, I explain about our last, and only meeting in Olesk. "You said if we ever met again, things wouldn't go as well for me."

Dai Li unfastens her cloak. She sits and crosses her legs, likely only to look less threatening.

"I was having a bad day."

"Getting caught in the middle of a Red Cuff massacre will do that." That day at the café with the green door is horrible to think about, so I change the subject. "Are we waiting for Mrs. Petrescu?"

"I expect we can start without her. She will need time with her husband."

"So he doesn't know?"

"Know what?"

A wry smile cracks my lips. So she's going to be cagey with me. I sit down in the chair furthest from Dai Li and prop the briefcase on my lap. "What's inside the orb?" I ask.

"Something important, but I don't know what."

I can't tell if she's lying. I'm sure "something important" is the truth, but I can't tell if she knows what it is.

"Do you know how to open it?"

"Put in the right combination."

"You're not going to tell me it, are you?"

"And why would I do that," Dai Li says, "when I still don't know where your loyalties lie?" The corners of her mouth rise slightly.

What does she know? "I've always been clear on that. Why would anything change?"

"A man's perspective on life and loyalty can change with the circumstances," she says with a shrug.

Before Olesk, I would never have questioned the Empire or my role in it. Since Olesk, I've had … doubts. And it's more than the cryptic, revolutionary mumbo I was fed in Olesk. It's been nothing singularly concrete; more a growing body of evidence that seems … off, for lack of a better word. I'm not the only one to sense it, either. R expressed doubts when I saw her in Tanev. R, of all people. She has always been a rock, the face of the Empire for me. She carries the commands down from the Emperor himself, or so it always seems. Yet she said she felt cut out of the loop. I was asked in Olesk if I knew who I worked for. At the time, I did. Now, I'm not so certain anymore, especially after the Red Cuffs set me up, and The Order seemed to know nothing about it, or did nothing to warn me.

"Tell me about the Silver Tigers and what happened in Olesk."

"There is little to tell," Dai Li says.

"How about starting with what are you?"

"I'm a concerned citizen, nothing more."

"Who hangs out in bars that get shot up by the Red Cuffs?"

"A hazard of the times," she says.

"That's not good enough."

"You're right, it's not."

Her response startles me so much that I lose my train of thought. I sit with my mouth hanging open.

"You deserve to know, considering what has

transpired recently. Alexei—you remember Alexei, yes?"

I nod. Alexei is dead, killed during the Red Cuff raid on the Green Door Café—the massacre from which only Dai Li and I escaped through good fortune. While he never said it at the time, I learned later that he and Dai Li had been working together to gather information about The Order, and specifically me.

"Alexei was right when he said you need to learn some things for yourself to believe them. I think you're starting to understand that. That said, I can tell you about the Silver Tigers. We're not revolutionaries. We don't seek to destroy the Empire or depose the Emperor. Our target is much bigger."

"Bigger?" What is bigger than the Empire? "World domination?" I hadn't meant to say it aloud, but in my surprise, I said the only thing I could think of bigger than the Empire.

Dai Li smiles, amused at my outburst.

My ears flush hot.

"No, not world domination," she says. "We're after The Order."

The Order? But that's not bigger than the Empire. I chuckle at her then raise my hand as if to say 'give me a second while I recover from your ridiculous joke.'

"You are clueless," she says.

"You're the one lacking perspective. The Order—"

"Extends beyond the Empire," she says.

"No."

She arches an eyebrow at me.

"We are agents of the Empire."

"True," Dai Li concedes, "to an extent. You are

also agents to a higher power that allows you to be subservient to the Emperor as long as that remains consistent with its goals."

"There is no higher power."

Dai Li shrugs, and her lack of argument reminds me of the words Alexei said to me in Olesk. Yet, this makes no sense. I *am* a servant of the Empire, and I do the bidding of the Emperor. The Order is beneath him, and we are loyal servants of the White Throne.

"You don't trust me enough to believe anything I say," Dai Li says.

"I don't trust anyone anymore."

"Good. That's the first step to learning the truth."

We sit for a moment in silence as I try to process what she's told me. Still, even with time to think on it, I can't wrap my head around it all. "I don't understand," I say. "Why send Carlo to help me, when you've tried several times to kill me? Why not let Krauss do it for you? You did send Carlo, yes?"

She sniffs derisively. "Krauss is a misogynistic bastard, but that has no bearing on your question." She pauses then, her lips pressing into a thin line, and for a moment I see something falter in her demeanor, a crack that reveals something beneath the stony façade she wears. "I assume Carlo is dead?" She looks down at her hands, and in that moment, she recomposes herself. When she looks up, she is Dai Li again. "You asked about the Silver Tigers, but there is more to that story. Recently there has been a schism within our group over how to achieve our goals—"

"Of destroying The Order?"

She glares at me, her mouth pressed together hard enough to leave wrinkles in her upper lip. "Most of our group still believes Valentin's approach is best.

They want everyone in The Order dead—"

"The guy on the train," I say.

Dai Li's brow folds into a series of wrinkles.

"You don't know anything about that? I nearly lost an ear on the train from Kovrov."

"I know nothing about that, but due to some carelessness in St. Stephensburg, you are a known commodity, so it only makes sense Valentin would have you targeted. Valentin and those who support him want the entire structure of The Order torn down, from the very top to the lowest man. Some few of us—Alexei, me, some others—believe there is a better way that doesn't require so much blood. When Catherine learned you had been taken by the Red Cuffs, we arranged to get Carlo inside to help."

"You mean to get the orb."

"That is just a fortunate bonus."

The response is not what I expected. My rescue was Carlo's objective, not the orb? No matter the story she's just told me, I find that hard to believe.

"And what of Mrs. Petrescu?" I ask. "I notice her name missing from your list of loyal friends."

"To be honest, I don't know. She claims to be on our side, but I have doubts. She and Valentin have a great deal of history, and trust has always been a difficult concept for me."

I understand her sentiment. Anyone in my line of work is either suspicious or dead, and trust isn't an essential element to either of those.

"Then whose orb is this?"

"Mine."

She says it quickly, and I can't tell for certain if she is lying, but looking at the artifacts cluttering Catherine Petrescu's sitting room, I do not believe her. Then I realize it doesn't matter because I'm not surrendering the orb to Dai Li, Catherine, or anyone else. The only question is what sort of deal I will need to make to get it opened.

"Do you know the combination?"

Dai Li settles back in the chair and crosses her arms. I suspect she's trying to figure out the best answer, be it the truth or otherwise. Before she can say anything, a commotion erupts in the hallway, a series of loud bangs and then the crash of splintering wood.

I jump to my feet, nearly launching the briefcase across the room. I grab it in mid-air.

Voices now, loud and aggressive, fill the hallway outside. An argument starts, but I can't identify the participants in the clatter of noise.

Dai Li cracks the door and shuts it quickly. "It's Krauss. He must have followed you."

"Impossible," I say, ready to argue with her. If Krauss followed me he would have stormed the house much sooner. I've been here at least twenty minutes, perhaps longer. If he followed anyone, it was Dai Li, but just as probable, he and Katalin guessed this as a likely destination for me.

Dai Li crosses to the blackout curtains.

"Not that way!" I say. "Krauss will have people posted outside." I wedge a chair under the door latch to buy us additional seconds. It won't hold for long, but there's nothing better.

Scanning the room, I see nothing that would serve as an effective weapon. We may need to go out the window after all. That would give us a better chance than staying here.

Dai Li is in the corner, running her fingers along

the top edge of the wainscoting. "I learned this from someone in Olesk," she says with a grin in my direction. "There's always another way." Her fingers catch on something, releasing a mechanism, and she pushes on the wall. The lower half swings away into a dark tunnel.

I'm unable to hide my surprise. Tunnels have always been a way in the Empire, especially in the old manors where it was advantageous to move around unobserved.

"Don't look too surprised. Catherine told me about the tunnels once. She says the ground beneath the city is riddled with them."

The knob rattles and the door knocks against the chair. "Open up in the name of the Emperor!" It seems only a moment passes before the men outside are shouldering the door.

Dai Li has already disappeared into the tunnel. I crouch before the opening. Just inside is a steep flight of stone stairs descending into blackness. I catch a glimpse of Dai Li as the darkness swallows her.

The pounding on the door increases.

I crawl through the opening, push the secret door shut behind me, then start down the steps after Dai Li, case in hand. Almost immediately, it's so dark I cannot see. I use my feet to find the edges of the steps and continue to slowly descend. After about thirty steps, the stairway bends and spirals down deeper into the rock.

I continue downward. The air grows cold and stale. I'm almost ready to turn back and take my chances hiding inside the secret door when a faint light colors the curved wall. Another bend and the stairs open into a small, roughly square chamber with brick walls.

In two of the walls, metal grilles block dark passageways. On the third are three torches in a rack.

Dai Li holds a lit torch aloft as she studies one of the grilles.

"Do you know the way?" I ask.

"No, but I suspect either will lead to a way out." The latch groans noisily as she springs it. The squeak of the hinges sends a shiver shooting through me.

"Maybe we should wait until they leave." The air in the chamber is not nearly as cold as outside, but it reminds me of the cell in which I spent too much time. The walls feel too close around me, making it hard to breathe. I'm not sure how long I can stay down here.

"Shhh!" Dai Li listens from the base of the steps. "Did you secure the door?" she whispers.

"Of course I did," I whisper hoarsely.

"Well, someone's coming down."

"Petrescu?"

"Do you want to wait to find out?"

"Lead the way."

I follow her into the dark passageway. The torchlight dances off the walls; Dai Li's shadow flickers around in the orange light.

"Wait," I say.

Dai Li pauses while I try to pull the grille shut without it making a noise. The hinges are too rusted, however, so I pull it quickly, deciding it's more important to close the grille than leave it open and give away down which of the two tunnels we went.

Dai Li moves quickly now, and the chamber fades into the blackness behind us. I'm thankful when the tunnel bends and slopes downward. The corner should hide our torchlight, if it hasn't already been seen.

Dug centuries ago, tunnels like these served many purposes, depending on the city and the times: catacombs, sewers, smuggling routes, and escape routes—any of a dozen purposes. I suspect Coruşu's tunnels were now reserved for people like Petrescu and kept operational in case the war were to turn suddenly sour.

After several minutes of feverish walking, I'm winded, and Dai Li is pulling ahead, taking the light with her. I call out to her, and she stops to wait for me. "Let me carry that," she says, reaching for the case. It weighs heavily on my arm, but I pull it away from her hand.

I put my finger to my lips. Just above the crackling of Dai Li's torch, footsteps echo faintly in the tunnel behind us. I stifle a curse. Dai Li hears them too; her eyes have a hunted look.

We continue on, sloping and twisting downward. I'm torn as to whether we should move silently or simply run for it. Dai Li seems to have a settled on a pace somewhere between the two.

The corridor levels out and runs straight now. I try to gauge how far we've descended and in what direction we're moving, but without visual cues, I'm unable to do either.

Several side corridors now come to meet our tunnel. Some of them have grillwork gates blocking them, similar to the one below the Petrescu manor. Others are open brickwork passages that delve quickly off into the dark. A few open onto stairs that drop even farther downward.

"I see light ahead," Dai Li says. She quickens her pace.

I've been sweating heavily since entering the tunnels, but now my sweat grows cold as the air temperature plummets. With every step, the tunnel grows lighter.

Dai Li stops suddenly, and I nearly run into her. She looses a distinctly crude curse.

Bars block the tunnel, and the grille door has a thick chain and padlock holding it closed. On the other side of the bars is a ladder that climbs to a grating through which daylight now streams in watery shafts. I tug at the chain, my panic rising.

"We have to go back. Try a side tunnel." Dai Li is already retracing our path into the darkness.
Reluctantly I follow. We move quickly now, fueled by a growing panic that we will meet Krauss and his men before we can get back to any of the open side passages.

"Stop!"

The voice echoes down the corridor from in front of us. Krauss's men from the sound of it. I can't see how many are there, only the bright flame of Dai Li's torch and the black of the tunnel beyond. Instead of obeying, Dai Li lowers her shoulders and rushes forward. I follow, but I'm unable to keep pace and fall behind. I pass an opening in the tunnel to my left, but Dai Li hasn't taken it, choosing instead to charge the Red Cuffs. Maybe she didn't see the tunnel? But she's too far ahead for me to stop her.

A shiver wracks me to the core, and for a moment, Dai Li's receding torch stutters to a stop as the world comes aligned. I see them then, suspended in the orange glow of the flames, glints of metal, like fireflies trapped in amber—freezing, starting, freezing again— as they move toward me. I throw myself against the brick wall as the world comes back on track and lurches forward. The flecks streak forward and the flechettes whistle by me. Dai Li cries out and tumbles to the ground, her torch sparking as it skitters across the floor.

Two Red Cuffs with a torch cautiously approach her. I edge forward, thinking I can surprise them, but then Krauss steps into the torchlight, his pistol still raised.

I stop in mid-step, holding still so I don't make a sound. I'm just out of the torchlight, I think. Krauss hasn't shot, so he must not see me.

Dai Li doesn't move, and I fear she's dead, until she emits a faint groan. One of the Red Cuffs kneels to check her. The other looks around nervously. Neither has his weapon drawn. Krauss ignores them, his eyes searching toward me. His pistol still raised, he edges down the passageway, his boots scraping on the ground in the dark. He crouches and picks up Dai Li's torch.

My knuckles ache from gripping the briefcase handle. Any moment he will see me, but even knowing this, I can't get my legs to move.

When his eyes widen suddenly, my paralysis is broken. I spin as flechettes splinter off the brick. A fragment cuts my cheek, feeling like a wasp sting, but otherwise harmless. Several more flechettes whistle by as I weave down the passageway. I turn into the opening I passed earlier, and plunge down the steps into the darkness. Fear screams through my body as I careen through the black. At any moment, I am going to smash into a wall so hard I will knock myself out, or I'll miss a step and tumble to down, breaking my neck. Instead, my foot comes up short as the stairs end. Pain shoots through my leg into my hip, and I tumble to the stone floor. The briefcase slams the ground next to me, but I keep my grip on it as I tumble over several times in the dark and splash down into a deep puddle of water.

I sit up quickly, my head spinning. The water in which I'm sitting flows swiftly around me; if it had been more than a hand's breadth deep, it would have carried me away. It's so cold it numbs the pain in my hip almost immediately.

Krauss's light outlines the passage I came down. It grows brighter as he nears.

The tunnel floor is concave and the water runs in the low spot toward a faint light in the distance. A way out or another dead end? I don't have time to decide.

I stumble to my feet. My head throbs, and I'm not sure if it's from the cold water, or if I hit it when I fell. Near the wall, the floor is dry, and I can move more quickly and quietly. I should probably move away from light, but I want to get out of these tunnels.

Krauss splashes into the water behind me.

I run faster. In the growing light I can better see the floor. It's closely fitted stones, slimy near the edge of the flowing water.

Krauss's light is a dozen meters behind me, but moving quickly. The muscles in my legs hurt. Any moment I fear they will seize up, and send me tumbling to the ground. The air gets colder with each step I take.

Please don't be blocked!

That's all that pounds through my head in time with the thudding of my deadened legs on the ground.

Don't be blocked. Don't be blocked.

The point of light grows brighter as the diameter of the tunnel shrinks. The opposite wall moves closer until I'm forced into the moving water. I use the walls to keep my balance on the slick stones. The ceiling descends until I have to crouch to keep going.

The opening ahead is a flat disc of gray, but it looks unblocked by any grating. My spirit leaps. If I can just get to it, I have a chance to elude Krauss.

Krauss splashes into the water behind me.

When I get to the opening, the ground disappears in front of me, and the water from the tunnel cascades off the lip, dropping seven meters into a fast-flowing river. I grab at the rough stonework, frantically trying to find a hold that will keep me from tumbling off into the icy water. My fingers grate on the brickwork before catching a protruding piece of masonry. My shoulder jerks back violently while my lower body continues forward and my entire weight snaps onto my arm. I splash down into the water cascading out the spillway. Sputtering and clawing, I gain purchase before the flow can carry me over the edge. I struggle to my knees, gripping the brickwork at the mouth of the tunnel. My left foot hangs off into space, and if I let go, without a doubt, I will be swept away.

"Nowhere to go," Krauss says. He's discarded the torch and braces himself against the flow of the water. He points his FP at me.

Why hasn't he shot me yet? Could I have been wrong about the orb? I clutch the briefcase to my chest. "Shoot me and you lose the orb."

Krauss licks his lips. "I don't care."

I believe him. I'm sure he would like to have the orb back, but he would gladly trade it for me. There can only be one reason he hasn't shot me yet. "What will Katalin say?"

"I don't care what she says."

The speed and force with which he answers tells me he might not care, but he also resents that she's the one calling the shots in this operation, and for whatever reason, he's compelled to obey her, and she wants me alive, not dead.

Krauss takes a cautious step closer.

I edge back, but there's nowhere to go. My feet are numb and my body shakes. Down below the river churns as it tumbles through the gorge. One of Coruşu's bridges arches overhead. This drainage conduit opens beneath it, hidden from public view. The steep sides of the gorge leave no dry land below. If I go over the side, I go into the river. I go to my death.

I've heard others talk about the no-win scenario, but winning or not winning is a product of one's perspective. Either of my choices likely results in my death, but one of them denies the Red Cuffs, and Krauss, specifically, the satisfaction of doing the deed himself. It also denies them the orb. But who wins by denying the Red Cuffs? The Silver Tigers, one or both groups of them? I don't know, but keeping the orb from the Red Cuffs at least leaves some chance it will find it way to somewhere it will do some good. Too many unknowns to consider while staring down the barrel of Krauss's FP. What is easy to determine is that one scenario allows Krauss personal satisfaction while the other does not, and given the general crappiness of my situation, I'll take the latter outcome as a personal victory.

I spring backward, clutching the briefcase tightly to my chest. The fall feels as if it takes several seconds. In my slow fall, I see all the details of the winter morning: the way the newly risen sun glints off the ice riming the leafless bushes along the shore, the cracks in the stonework arch, the black hole of the drainage tunnel framing Krauss's shocked expression.

I hit the water, and it closes in on me, slamming against my ears. It's like a huge fist punches me in the chest; all the air is forced from my lungs by the shock and pressure of the cold. My skin is on fire, and if I hadn't been concentrating so hard on holding onto the case, I would have lost it on impact.

I struggle back to surface, breaking through the white water. The bridge is well behind me as the current carries me swiftly downstream. I have only seconds before I succumb to the cold, but with only one free hand and the briefcase acting like an anchor, it is difficult to make way against the current. I cannot let the briefcase go, however, no matter how much sense it might make. Whatever is inside the Celestial Orb, it's as important as my life right now.

Repeatedly water washes over my head and each time, I'm certain I will never come up, but somehow I manage to struggle back to the surface. The burning sensation has subsided, and the feeling in my toes is gone. I continue to struggle for the bank, which as I flow out of the narrow gorge near the bridge, slopes gently up from the river's edge. The river bends ahead, and I'm washed into a slow spot. My feet catch on the bottom, but I can't feel if it's a rock or tree snag. I struggle closer to the shore. My vision has gone frosty at the edges. I can no longer focus on anything except the rocks in front of me as I haul myself one-armed up onto the bank where I collapse in the snow.

Steam pours from my body. My breath rises in a frost geyser. I shake uncontrollably.

The briefcase is still clutched in my hand. I should have let it go because now Krauss will find it when he finds my body, frozen to the rocks. I try to throw it back into the stream, but my arm doesn't respond.

My vision goes white, like an interrogation lamp is in my face, but instead of the heat from an incandescent bulb, I feel nothing. The cold has passed, and I know this is the end.

Voices call to me through the mist, and I vaguely recognize them from my past but can't identify who they are. Alive or dead. Male or female. I want to call to them, but cannot.

Then my body rises into the lightness.

I AWAKE IN A COCOON of warmth with a memory of voices and shadows. Everything is hazy gray and quiet except for a methodical ticking. A slit opens in the gray like a cut in fabric, behind which hides a room.

The slit widens as my eyes open.

The ticking comes from a mantel clock on the table next to my bed. The only other thing I can see over the stack of blankets piled on my chest is my long coat and the hat I took from the train in Coruşu draped on a coat rack in the corner. But this isn't my room at the Petresi, and trying to sort out how my coat and hat came to be here only makes my head hurt.

I move my legs, and it's like priming a pump, except it pulls forth a groan instead of water. I hurt, a deep hurt like a bruise that goes all the way to center of my bones.

A rustling noise and then a woman's gravelly voice: "Welcome back, Mr. Petrenko."

A silver-haired matriarch slides into my field of vision. I've never seen her before, and she addresses

161

me with my most commonly used cover name.

"Wh—" I start, but my throat is so dry it won't open to let the words out.

"Don't talk," the woman says.

She helps me sit up, and gives me a cup with chips of ice in it. Absently, I wonder if they are from the windowsill; it's crusted so heavily the city outside is distorted into abstraction.

My arms are too weak to put the cup to my lips, so the woman does it for me.

"You're safe." Her voice is reassuring, like a soothing tonic.

But there is something I want to know only I can't remember what it is. My face pulls into a grimace; the skin crinkled along the corners of my eyes hurts.

The woman pats my arm. "Don't worry; your case is here, too."

Good, I think, but I can't remember why that's good. The case is important—of that I am certain—but I don't know why.

"Lord knows you weren't going to lose it. They had to pry it from your hands."

"They?" I can manage only the single word. My throat hurts.

"Now is not the time."

No, now is the time! But when I try to grab the woman's elbow, my arm is too heavy to even lift and my hand flops back onto the blanket. My wrist is wrapped in bandages.

"Rest now," she says. "We will talk later." She slides me back down under the covers. I am too weak to resist, even though my mind spins with questions. I try to speak again, but nothing comes out, and I am powerless to compel answers from her. My efforts, as futile are they are, leave me exhausted, and sleep quickly overtakes me once again.

今

I WAKE SEVERAL TIMES over the next few days.
Always the silver-haired woman is there as if she's
holding vigil over me. She brings food; at first a thin
broth that is flavorful if salty, but soon after more
substantial fare—sour soups with chunks of meat,
bread, cutlets. These fill my stomach and rebuild my
strength. The pain in my body fades with the bruises
and the cuts. The bandages on my wrists are
removed, revealing bracelets of scabs.

When I can speak without pain, the woman—she
tells me her name is Ioana, but for some reason I
suspect that's not her real name—talks with me, but
she speaks only about her grandchildren and the
failings of her numerous relations. Whenever I start
to raise other potentially pricklier subjects, she
skillfully redirects the conversation. After several
failed attempts, I confront her about it.

"You are not a prisoner," she says. "The door locks
on this side only; you can walk out it anytime you like,
but I suggest you get your strength back first."

She's right, so I resign myself to getting stronger,

so I can find my own answers.

Soon the scabs begin to slough away, the bruises that purpled my legs and chest fade, and I am able to get out of bed, at first for short periods, but longer with each passing day. She discourages me from leaving the room ("I'm not strong enough to carry you back here"), so I walk around the modest-sized room working strength back into my legs and guessing answers to my numerous questions.

Ioana must work for The Order, directly or indirectly. The presence of my long coat is proof of that, or at least I convince myself of that truth. R must be behind this. Surely she must have dispatched my mysterious rescuers, but how did they find me, and with such fortuitous timing? More importantly, why did it take them so long?

The briefcase with the Celestial Orb sits next to the coat rack. Once I am strong enough, I spend the evenings after Ioana leaves sitting on my bed, the case open before me. I don't touch the orb, I just stare at it, as if I'm afraid it will vanish if it comes in contact with my skin. Like everything else, it offers me no answers.

After six days, Ioana declares me fit, and instead of a nightshirt, she brings me fresh clothes and shoes. Tucked into the suit coat's breast pocket is an envelope. It has no writing on the outside and no postage.

"There is *papricaş* on the stove downstairs," she says. "I am going now." She smiles warmly at me, and before I can thank her adequately for everything she has done, she leaves. From the window, I watch her disappear down the alley.

Inside the envelope is a train ticket to Aurestapol.

今

AFTER ALL THAT HAS HAPPENED, I have been
changed. I notice it when I step onto the platform at
Aurestapol's Grand Station. Once a testament to the
greatness of the Empire, now it feels threatening,
huge, like a great mouth ready to swallow me. I stand
on the platform, my heart pounding as the other
passengers push past me and up the stairs to the
lobby.

I force down the lump in my throat. As I come up
the stairs from the platform, the great dome sweeps
upward into blue shadows overhead. Civilians and
soldiers pack the wide concourse watching the clacker
boards with a cold intensity. The Armistice clock
chimes out the fifteenth hour, a sharp metallic sound
that chills my heart.

I pull the collar of my long coat tighter around my
throat. My left hand tightens on the handle of the
briefcase.

I head toward the exit. As I pass the tables outside
of the station's café, a voice cuts through the noise.

"Calypto!"

I stop and scan the people in drab winter coats at the café tables. My eyes stop on R.

She motions to me and nods toward the chair across from her.

I should be surprised to see her, but I'm not. I sit across from her, placing the briefcase on the ground between my feet.

"How did you know?" I ask. I have already guessed she is responsible for the ticket, but it was an open return, and I did not contact her from Coruşu with my schedule. How could she know I would use the ticket today?

"You shouldn't have come back here, Calypto," she says, ignoring my question.

My brow pinches together. "You gave me a ticket."

"I knew you would come anyway," she says with a shrug. "So it might as well be on my schedule so I could be sure to intercept you."

"But back to my first question, how—"

"I've had coffee here at this time every day since I sent the ticket."

A simple answer, indeed, and I should have seen it. The ticket date may have been open, but the route is not. She knew I would be on this train, just not the date.

"And how did you find me in Coruşu?"

R waves her hand, dismissing my question. I grab her hand to stop the motion, catching her off guard. Surprise is evident on her face.

She draws back her hand from mine. "You have more friends than you realize, and they seem to have less sense than you do. Fortunately for you, they have a talent for seeing things that most cannot."

"Lera?"

R's lips pinch together as if she's just sucked on a lemon. "Defiant ... but in a good way. Smart, too, how she covered her trail. Birdie helped, but you didn't hear that from me or anyone else."

"Did—"

"Enough questions; they only waste what little time we have. Another train leaves in thirty minutes from platform eight." She slides a ticket across the table to me. "Be on it."

Automatically I look for a mission envelope on the table, but there isn't one.

"An auto will be waiting at your final destination." The key comes next. It scrapes across the tabletop and sits now in front of me. "It's yours. Go wherever you want as long as it's far from here, and no one knows you."

"But—"

She doesn't let me speak yet. She slides one more thing to me: a white envelope stuffed with crisp bills. "That should be enough to get you back on your feet."

"I don't understand." I leave the envelope on the table. I don't even look at it; instead I stare into R's face. Her expression is unreadable, however. "This isn't a mission, is it?"

"But it is, and I believe the most important one you may ever do."

Now I'm confused, and it must show on my face.

"Things bigger than us are happening, and somehow, you have found your way into the center of it all."

"The Silver—"

R holds up her hand. "As best I can tell, they are only one player. I've tried to learn more, but ..." She

169

shakes her head, and I don't know exactly what that means. She hasn't been able to find out? She's been stopped from finding out?

I think about what Dai Li told me in Coruşu. Other than R, and a few field operatives like myself, I really don't know anyone in the Order. As an organization, we operate from the shadows, which I believe is a necessity given what we do.

"I can't help feeling this last mission was no mistake," R says.

"What do you mean?"

"You weren't meant to come back."

"A set-up?" The words hit me like a crowbar. "Who?"

R shakes her head. "I don't know, and my sources have dried up."

I lay the briefcase on the table. "I think this is the key to some of those answers."

R looks from me to the case and then back to me.

I unsnap the latches, but R puts her hand on the lid and stops me from opening it.

"The less I know the better," she says. "I think that case is safest with you. For now."

The clock in the center of the concourse chimes the quarter hour. "You better get going," she says. "Your new mission, Calypto, is to stay alive until you are needed again."

"How will I know?"

A sly smile crosses her face. "I have a friend named Osip who sells antique stand lamps through the classifieds in the Sunday *Gazeta*. I think you might find his offers of interest."

I nod, but to be honest, I don't know what to do. R is sending me away, but on what sort of mission and for whom? It doesn't take special training to see this is not an official mission. She is getting me out of Aurestapol, out of danger. Will she ever send word to come back? The thickness of the envelope on the table says that is unlikely, but I have always trusted her, and now is no time to stop.

"What are you going to do?" I ask, stuffing the envelope of money into my coat pocket.

"Return to what I do. Try to learn everything I can. And pray for you." She stands up.

I fumble out of my chair. We shake hands; R has a firm grip.

"This mission is over, Calypto; you did a good job. Now stay alive because before all this is over, I believe you will have a role to play."

She leaves me standing at the table, and disappears into the crowd.

今

THE TRAIN PLOWS its way north across the Empire's
central plain. It's a desolate area, especially in the
winter when it's a sheet of white snow dotted
sporadically with small farm houses and grain silos.
Occasionally we pass through a town, but there's
nothing of substantial size between Aurestapol and
my destination, seven hours away.

I grow bored of looking out the window, and the
endless, but unproductive, churning of my thoughts
won't let me sleep. My compartment is empty and the
shade on the door secured, so I remove the orb and
set aside the briefcase. The orb is warm in my hands,
much like the last time I held it. That must be a trick
of my imagination because it can't be generating its
own heat, but the sensation is unsettling whether it's
all in my head or not.

Also like that last time, I still have no idea how to
open it.

My first thought is to smash it. It looks delicate
enough that a few stout blows with a hammer or on
the compartment floor should do it. But not knowing

the nature of its secret, I might ruin whatever answers it holds for me.

"No," I whisper to the orb, holding it up close to my lips. "I have to open you."

The possible combinations are infinite. Yet, I am fairly certain that Catherine Petrescu must have been intended to open it, so she must have known the combination, or at least have been able to guess it. If they had been able to share information directly and easily, then why go through the trouble of using the orb? So the date must be something Petrescu could have reasonably guessed. What's a date that would have had meaning to her and would have been known by whoever sent it?

I spin the rings idly as I think. Birthdays, holidays ... so many choices ... historical moments, weddings, graduations ... I pause. Weddings. At the auction, Petrescu had mentioned their wedding anniversary, and the way they doted over each other after all these years, particularly Catherine, tells me this is an important date. I dredge the memories of that night with some difficulty, but eventually remember that they had been married on Coronation Day.

The rings move smoothly and quietly as I rotate them into the right position, but the date combination doesn't open the orb. Then I realize that the date isn't correct. The Petrescus weren't married on the day of the Emperor's actual coronation. They had been married before that ... but how long ago was it? Forty years, I recall suddenly.

I rotate the rings.

Nothing.

With a sigh, I set the orb in my lap, and let my mind wander through other dates. I try a few halfheartedly and without success.

The auction card peeks out at me from inside the open briefcase. Retrieving it, I study it again for any clue. The crafting date catches my attention—early eighteenth century. What would that mean for dates? Nothing, unless ... I sit up with a jolt. The Latin alphabet suggests the orb's creator is not from the Empire. That would mean the craftsman would have used the Gregorian calendar, not the Julian. If the orb had come from the Papalate, then the sender would likely use the Gregorian calendar, too. Romani, prior to joining the Empire had also adopted the Gregorian calendar, so Catherine Petrescu, a daughter of a Romani noble family would be well versed in it.

I wrack my brain trying to remember how to convert between the two. Ten days were added by Pope Gregory, but there were also some other rules implemented to keep the calendar properly aligned and I don't know them. They were small adjustments, however, and they couldn't total more than a few days. I add twelve days to the Petrescus' anniversary and spin the rings to align the numbers.

My breath catches as I hear a faint click. The two halves of the orb split, but instead of being hinged like box, they rotate on a peg. The seam had been hidden along the edge of one of the rings.

The inside of the orb is mostly solid, except for a small rectangular compartment into which a stoppered phial has been wedged. With trembling fingers, I pry it loose. Something white shifts around the inside when I tilt the phial to and fro. It looks like ... sand?

I turn the orb over and give it a shake, hoping something more will fall out, but nothing does. I set the orb back into its foam packing.

All this for sand? I squeeze the phial in my fist, barely able to contain a scream of outrage, but that passes quickly, and I'm flooded with disappointment.

Sand!

I push the phial deep into the pocket of my long coat. As I do, my sleeve rides up revealing the pink scars around my wrists. All that for a phial of sand?

I stare out the window at the endless white plain. I don't want to think about any of this any longer. Maybe R is right; it's time for me to slip away quietly into the night.

To hell with the sand.

To hell with the past.

I close my eyes and the white world disappears, but instead of peace in the blackness, I imagine a beach.

End of Book Two

Thank you for reading Book Two of the Calypto Cycle. Gaining exposure as an independent author relies mostly on word-of-mouth, so if you have the time and inclination, please consider leaving a short review wherever you can.

MEET THE AUTHOR

D. Thomas Minton writes from his home in the Pacific Northwest of the United States, where he lives a short walk from vineyards and alpaca farms. When not writing, he travels to remote locations and helps communities across the Pacific Ocean protect coral reefs. His stories have appeared in some of science fiction's top publications. He can found online at dthomasminton.com.

A sneak peek at
Threads Unravel
Book Three of the Calypto Cycle

I SQUINT GRITTY-EYED into the near whiteout. To
fight the landscape's trancelike quality, I force myself
to imagine my future life, but I cannot. The white
world is overpowering, and it tugs at my focus as
much as my fortitude. I should have stayed in
Peskovyka another night, but the woman at the guest
house had said a storm was coming—she could feel it
in her swollen knuckles—and if I didn't want to get
stuck there, I had best try to outrun it. A poor
choice, I realize now as I wipe at my stinging eyes. I
will stop in the next town, but if past experience is
any indication, I won't reach that until after nightfall.
I've seen only a dozen turnoffs since leaving
Peskovyka four hours ago, and most of these were
gravel ways winding across the snowy plain to
crumbling manors whose families likely reach back
dozens of generations.

Over the past hour, the pitch of the auto's flywheel
engine has dropped. The last two spin stations I've
passed were shuttered tightly against the winter. Now
I am worried the spin will run down. Then I'll really

be stuck.

I jolt awake again right before I slam into a dark shape in the road. I jerk the wheel and skid across the packed ice and drifting snow, sliding into the frozen grass before shuddering to a stop.

Had that been something actually in the road or a snow hallucination?

I turn, looking out the narrow back window rimed with ice, but it's a plate of white. I disengage the flywheel and set the brake.

The grass crunches under my shoes as I climb out. Wind whips my hair. I haven't cut it in months, and I have twisted it into short locs as I lay in bed at night.

My auto looks undamaged, and the frozen ground should allow me to get it back on the road without difficulty.

Several meters behind my auto is another vehicle and a woman standing next to it, her red scarf snapping in the wind like a pennant.

"Are you okay?" she yells at me. I barely hear her over the wind.

"I didn't see you until the last minute," I say. She's lucky to be standing.

"I was afraid I would miss anyone who came along," she says.

That makes sense. I haven't seen a single auto since leaving Peskovyka. No one with any sense would be out here in this weather. That thought makes my neck tingle. Is it coincidence that I nearly hit her on the road?

My FP is a warm lump in its holster under my right arm. I'm tempted to unbutton my coat, but it's very cold, and if she is a threat that would give away any surprise I might have.

"My auto stopped running," she says.

She has her arms wrapped around herself so that I cannot clearly see her hands. Her scarf is iced with a crust of snow, except where her warm breath has melted it.

"A bad day to be on the road," I say.

"I was helping a sick neighbor." She doesn't carry herself like a potential threat, but that could be a sign of a professional. Her face is slender, and even in her bulky coat, I can tell she is not a large woman. In all her winter gear, I doubt she weighs fifty kilos.

"Your husband—"

"I don't have one. Not anymore."

She doesn't need to say anything more. The war has claimed many of the Empire's citizens—its sons, and brothers and fathers and husbands.

"Maybe I can help." I come forward cautiously. Her arms squeeze more tightly around her torso. If she is armed, it would be with a small, limited-shot pistol.

She retreats back to her auto, an older model that has seen better days. The body is dented with patches of rust. Based on the thickness of the snow on the windshield, she's been her an hour or more. The hood is folded back.

She motions toward the exposed engine with a gloved, but otherwise empty, hand

I relax some, but I don't allow myself to get complacent.

"It's spinning, but ..." She shakes her head.

I know almost nothing about engines, but I poke my head under the hood and ask her to engage the flywheel while I listen. The hum of the spinning wheel doesn't change and the engine makes an unsatisfying clicking noise, but the drive train doesn't engage. That's as much as I'm able to decipher, even if I'm not willing to admit it yet.

I tug a few cables to check their connections, but to be honest, I have no idea what any of them do. The pitch of the flywheel never changes.

A pair of lights emerges from the snow behind us and another auto rolls slowly out of the whiteout. It comes up along the side and stops. The windshield is fogged over on the inside, edged with frost on the outside. The passenger door opens.

"Oh look; someone else to help," the woman says.

Look for
Threads Unravel, Book Three of the Calypto Cycle
at an online vendor near you in 2018.